Ham

Wolfpack On The Prowl

by

G. E. Nolly

www.genolly.com

This book is a work of fiction. Names, characters, places and incidents are either the product of the author's imagination or are used fictionally. Any resemblance to actual persons, living or dead, or to actual events or locales is entirely coincidental.

ISBN 978-0-9754362-9-5

This book is dedicated to American military veterans, past, present, and future.

Version 2012.12.02

1

January 17, 1970

T-39 training was going well. I had received a quick local ground school, and was already well underway into my checkout.

The flight training had started two days earlier, with an extensive briefing and local landing practice mission each day, and today I flew from Yokota Air Base, in Japan, to Kunsan Air Base, in South Korea.

We had departed Yokota early, at 0500 local, and had arrived at Kunsan in time to get to the Officer's Club for breakfast. The mission was going flawlessly. I'd been studying T-39 systems and procedures on my own for the past couple weeks, and my preparation had paid off.

This was my cross-country training flight, from Yokota to Kunsan, with a return to Yokota planned for the same day. My IP, Lieutenant Colonel Byers, was an ex-fighter pilot, and we got along great. He briefed me on the particulars of our return trip while we ate, then we went to Base Ops to do our flight planning. With favorable winds, we'd be back at Yokota by early afternoon, and I'd have no problem meeting up with Samantha for dinner at the Yokota Officer's Club. A new band had just arrived from the States, and I was really looking forward to dancing with her again after we ate.

At the end of this trip, I'd be signed off to fly in a normal crew environment. I'd be a copilot for a while, but that was fine with me. I'd get to observe fully-qualified Aircraft Commanders during routine operations, and I would get a chance to hone my skills in the T-39. I would need at least 100 hours in the airplane before I could carry passengers, so the Ops Officer, Major Simmons, had scheduled me on the fast track to fly a lot of cross-country flights.

"You'll get experience flying into all the usual places we go," he'd said. "Kadena Air

Base, in Okinawa, Clark Air Base, in the Philippines, and all the bases in Korea. Once we get you passenger-qualified, we'll put you on some of our better missions, like Hong Kong. I think you're really going to like the variety of flying we have here, Hamilton."

It was kind of funny being called by my actual name, Hamilton, instead of the nickname I'd picked up in Vietnam – Hamfist. I figured as long as nobody knew me as Hamfist, I'd just wait to see what developed, name-wise. Hamilton was just fine with me.

After flight planning at Kunsan Base Ops, I zapped through the preflight and got down to engine start. But when I pressed the starter button on the first engine, nothing happened. We rechecked the switches and tried again. Nothing. Maintenance Staff Sergeant Adams, from Transient Alert, checked under the cowling and determined that the starter was bad on that engine. Naturally, there were no parts at Kunsan. It looked like we would be stuck there for the night. So much for dancing.

Then I got a brilliant idea. I knew my IP would be impressed with my knowledge of aircraft systems, as well as my resourcefulness.

"Why don't we start the other engine, then fast taxi down the runway?" I asked. "When we get enough windmilling airspeed, we go to AIRSTART on the bad engine and get it lit. Then we can take off and fly back to Yokota and get it fixed."

Lieutenant Colonel Byers took a long draw on his cigarette, looked up at the sky and then leveled his gaze at me.

"What do you see when you look up?" he asked.

I looked around.

"Nothing," I replied, "just blue sky."

“That's right. The sky is blue, it's a beautiful day, and we're in perfect health. We don't have a mission that requires us to trade that for an uncertain future and needless risks. The base isn't under attack. We're not taking a critically ill patient to emergency surgery. We're not even carrying passengers. We're on a training mission, and we're stuck at a place that really doesn't have a lot to offer, but that's the breaks - no pun intended. It's better to be on the ground wishing you were in the air, than in the air wishing you were back on the ground.”

He gave me a lot to think about. All of my operational flying, up until now, had been in combat. Lives, literally, depended on my getting the mission accomplished. And now it was different. Dinner and dancing with Sam would have to wait.

We got two rooms at the BOQ. It was a lucky break that my IP was a Field Grade officer. As a Company Grade officer, a First Lieutenant, I would normally be put in a two-man room with my IP. But since he was Field Grade, he got his own individual room, and I did also by default.

Lieutenant Colonel Byers managed to get an autovon call through to the Yokota Command Post, to tell them of our maintenance situation. The autovon was the military telephone system for international calls. The Command Post needed to know that our airplane would be out until the next day, and they would pass on our itinerary information to our families. Although Sam and I weren't married yet, she was listed as my emergency contact, so I knew they would call her.

We spent the night at Kunsan, and by morning the airplane was fixed.

2

January 18, 1970

The T-39 mission at Yokota Air Base was totally different from the flying I'd done in Vietnam. It was like a mini-airline operation for congressmen, Generals and other VIPs.

The T-39 Sabreliner was a small business jet, carrying seven passengers in real style. The T-39 jocks liked to point out that the airplane had the same wing as the vaunted F-86 fighter, and it handled somewhat like a fighter. And with its J60 turbojet engines, it had great acceleration. A real step up from the O-2A.

Our organization was not a real squadron, it was a part of Base Operations. We had four Sabreliner airplanes and ten assigned pilots. Then we had about 25 “attached” pilots who worked staff jobs at Fifth Air Force Headquarters and each flew a few days each month, frequently on weekends.

When we weren't flying, each of us assigned pilots had additional duties. Basically, we had to perform all the collateral duties that were performed by the hundred or so pilots in a normal squadron, so we stayed pretty busy with, well, busy-work.

Typically, we wore our blue uniforms when we flew. The uniform consisted of dark blue pants and a light blue short-sleeve shirt with no tie. We also had dark blue athletic jackets, similar to what the pilots of Air Force One had, to wear during cold weather. When it was extremely cold, we were authorized to wear the standard olive drab Air Force winter flying jacket, but it was pretty much frowned upon.

There was another facet of our mission that I found out about after I got into the unit, but it wouldn't apply to me until I was fully checked out. It turned out the Scatback T-39 operation in Vietnam was under-manned, and our unit provided pilots TDY – Temporary Duty – to Saigon for three months at a time. I had envisioned Yokota T-39 flying as being basically out-and-back one-day or two-day missions, and had thought I'd be home, with Sam, virtually every night. To say I was disappointed would be an understatement.

After my overnight at Kunsan, Sam and I had a long talk. I explained what I'd learned about the T-39 mission, and told her about the Scatback tasking. I wasn't sure what her response would be.

I shouldn't have been worried.

“Ham, you're doing your job. It's what you do. I know you volunteered for Yokota to be near me, and that means the world to me.”

Damn, I had really struck gold!

3

January 18, 1970

My car finally arrived. One of the first things I had done when I got my assignment changed to Yokota was call Morris's Motor Storage, where I had stored my Datsun while I was in Vietnam. I placed the call through the autovon. Mr. Morris had sounded really relieved to hear I had made it through my tour unscathed. No need to tell him about my injury.

I had arranged the shipment of my car through the Traffic Management Office, and they had scheduled the port-call. Mr. Morris had personally driven my Datsun to Oakland Port, and then sent me a telegram with the shipment information. He was really a good guy.

Sam went with me to pick up my car at Yokohama Port. It was a strange feeling sitting behind the wheel after my experiences of the last year. I finally understood the expressions, “You can't go home again” and “You can't bathe twice in the same river”. I had changed. I was a different person, and many of the things that had been important to me before I'd left for Vietnam now seemed trivial.

I looked over at Sam, sitting next to me. She was smiling.

“Nice car.”

“Yeah, but it's just a car. The important thing is you're sitting next to me.”

She reached over and grabbed my hand.

“Especially,” I smiled, “since I don't have a clue how to get back to Yokota, or how to drive on the wrong side of the road.”

“Don't worry, honey, I'll take care of you.”

It was comforting to have her next to me. I hoped I would have her next to me for the rest of my life.

4

February 5, 1970

Pre-marital counseling was a whole lot more than simply sitting down with a counselor and getting a briefing. It was work, hard work.

"I'll be giving you homework assignments, and I want you to know you'll only get out of this program what you put into it," explained Chaplain Mackay.

Our assignments required us to communicate, to makc lists, to argue. We had to have intense, intimate conversations about things I had never even considered.

Did we want children? If so, how soon? If so, what religion would they be brought up in, if any? What about discipline?

What was our attitude toward money? I knew Sam had grown up in a wealthy family, and had earned a lot of money modeling. I had grown up in a household that worried a lot about money. How would we handle money decisions? One bank account or two?

We had to learn how to argue.

“But we don't fight,” we protested.

“Everybody says that. But you will, trust me.”

So we had to learn the ground rules for constructive arguing. What words to use. What words to avoid. We learned to negotiate.

We had to make a list of things our parents did, as married couples, that we didn't want to repeat.

“And don't tell me your parents were perfect,” Chaplain Mackay said, “Nobody is.”

And we made lists of successful couples we wanted to use as role models. And it would be okay to use our own parents, if we wanted.

Most of all, we learned to nurture our

commitment to each other.

Sam was really resourceful at getting what she wanted. When she heard I would be flying a T-39 trip to Hong Kong and there would be empty seats on the plane, she figured out a way to go along. She found a law conference in Hong Kong for the same weekend, and convinced her boss that it would be beneficial if she could attend. Especially since there was an Air force plane going there anyway, so transportation would be free.

Flying into Kai Tak airport was a real challenge, and very rewarding. The IGS Approach to Runway 13 required homing to an ADF, then turning and intercepting what appeared to be an ILS, but it terminated with the airplane pointed at a checkerboard painted on the side of a hill.

When you broke out of the clouds and saw the checkerboard, you had to immediately initiate a hard right turn and descend immediately, just barely above the rooftops, to land on a short runway that ended at the water's edge. And the winds were always tricky.

It was a real pilot's approach. Anybody could fly a plain vanilla ILS. It took a real pilot to fly the IGS at Kai Tak.

We had a great time in Hong Kong. Sam dutifully attended the conference by day, and we went out at night. We did some shopping. We did some sightseeing. And we took the tram up to the Peak Restaurant and had a great dinner while we watched the Hong Kong harbor lights below us.

It was great to have Sam along when I was flying. I wanted her to see what I did for a living, and I wished I could have had her with me on every trip.

5

February 28, 1970

It was my turn in the barrel, to go TDY to the Scatback operation. It would be a 3-month assignment, and I'd be getting extra money in the form of combat pay, plus TDY pay. I'd also get an income tax deduction for every month I was in Vietnam. The schedulers arranged for our TDY assignments to start a day or two before the end of one month, and end a day or two after the beginning of the month 93 days later. That way we'd get combat pay and the combat tax deduction for five months.

This was going to be the first time I would be away from Sam for an extended period since we'd gotten engaged. I wasn't really sure how Sam, or I, would handle the separation.

The night before I left, Sam and I went to dinner with her parents, Tom and Miyako. It reminded me a lot of the time the four of us had waited at the snack bar for my flight to Vietnam after my R&R in Tokyo. But this time I wouldn't be leaving for six months. I'd only be gone for three months. But, again, I would be going back to Vietnam.

After dinner, Tom and Miyako went home, and Sam and I went to one of the numerous "love hotels" that are endemic to Japan. It was a beautiful, small *ryokan* with a romantic view. And we shared a wonderful, intimate night together. It was too short.

Just so there's no misunderstanding, it was the *night* that was too short!

6

March 5, 1970

I'd been in Vietnam for five days, and was getting used to being back in country. The sights, the sounds, and the smells brought back a familiar feeling.

Our flying was an eclectic mix of combat support missions, transporting reconnaissance imagery from one base to another, and VIP support, carrying high-ranking officers and Department of Defense personnel throughout Southeast Asia. We operated around the clock, with a major portion of our missions at night.

Among the T-39 pilots, I was known simply as Ham, although some called me Hamilton. The moniker Hamfist never reared its head.

Scatback headquarters was at Ton Son Nhut Air Base, in Saigon. Our Commander was Lieutenant Colonel Miller, and he seemed like a good guy. When I first arrived, I had a short meeting with him and the Operations Officer, Major Greene. After some brief introductions and small talk, Major Greene spoke.

“Lieutenant Hancock, we've been looking at your flying records, and we'd like to put you on the fast track to upgrade to Aircraft Commander. Are you comfortable with that?”

“Yes, sir. I feel pretty much at home in the Sabreliner now, and I'm very familiar with this theater of operations. Thank you for considering me.”

It was very unusual for a Lieutenant to be an Aircraft Commander, and I appreciated the vote of confidence. For the next week, I flew exclusively with Major Greene, and he did an outstanding job of teaching me the finer points of being in command of a passenger operation. At the end of the week, he signed me off as AC.

Unlike the VIP flights from Yokota, we didn't wear our blue uniforms when we flew, we wore nomex flight suits. That made sense. Even though we were often carrying high-ranking VIPs, we were in a combat environment, and function took priority over appearance.

7

May 5, 1970

We landed at Ton Son Nhut Air Base, in Saigon, early in the morning. We were scheduled to operate our next flight a little after midnight, so we went to the Billeting Office to get a room at the Visiting Officer's Quarters. They assigned me to an austere room with my Copilot, Captain Jack Emmers.

When we had first started the flight sequence, Jack seemed a bit uneasy being a Copilot to a Lieutenant, but he became more comfortable as the sequence wore on. I had no problem with it, of course, since I had been the pilot-in-command when I flew O-2 missions out of DaNang with Forward Air Navigators, some of whom were Majors. Air Force Regulation 60-1 was very specific about the pilot-in-command being in command, regardless of rank.

Jack was an attached pilot, and had requested this TDY. He hadn't yet had an assignment to Vietnam, and wanted to come over to support the war effort, as well as to get experience in a combat environment.

After we got settled, Jack suggested we head over to the Officer's Club for breakfast. We got a table near the patio, and ordered the breakfast buffet. I went over to the serving table and filled my plate from the sumptuous selection of food. No shortages here.

I returned to our table and started eating. There was a young Vietnamese kid wearing a white smock, maybe eight years old, moving from table to table, pouring coffee. I could see that he kept looking in my direction. Finally, he hesitantly walked up to my table.

“I happy.”

“I'm glad to hear that,” I said. I wasn't really sure how to respond. “We're here to help. I hope we can bring peace to your country.”

"No, I *Happy,*" he replied. "Happy, Dopey, Sleepy, Grumpy, Sneezy, Bashful, Doc. I Happy."

I looked at him carefully and did a double-take. I hadn't recognized him, in part, because the last time I had seen him he had been wearing an eye patch. Now he had a prosthetic eye. Yeah, I recognized him now. It was Happy, one of the kids I had gotten to know so well at Cam Ranh Bay!

Of all the kids I had played with at the Cam Ranh hospital, Happy was the one I felt closest to. When Grumpy had been killed in the sapper attack, Happy was the most affected of all the children. I was a bit surprised, since I had been certain that the kids would have become desensitized to the tragedy and death that was part and parcel of their everyday lives. I spent a lot of time with him trying to comfort him and help him adjust.

"Grumpy was Happy's brother," explained

Major Rader, the head nurse in the children's ward. "Grumpy was his last living relative. His parents were killed in the rocket attack that injured them, and we've been unable to locate any other family members. When he's well enough to leave the hospital, he'll be going to an orphanage in Saigon."

I stood up and gave him a big hug, and he hugged me back so hard I thought he wouldn't let go. I pulled back and looked at him.

"You've gotten so big," I said. "I hardly recognized you."

I don't think he understood much of what I said, but Happy just stood there and beamed.

The Vietnamese Club Manager came over to our table to see if everything was okay.

"Everything is fine," I answered. "We're old friends. How long has this young man been working here?"

"He here three month," the manager

answered. "He live in orphanage and he work here in daytime."

"Which orphanage?" I asked.

"He live Hoi Duc Anh Orphanage."

"What time does he get off work?" I asked.

"He leave at noon."

I ate breakfast and went up to Happy, who had kept looking at me and smiling the whole time.

"I'll be back here when you are finished work today," I said. I wasn't sure if he understood me, but it didn't matter.

I told Jack my plans, went back to the VOQ room, set an alarm, and took a power nap. At 1130 the alarm woke me, and I changed into fatigues and headed back to the O'Club.

It was time for me to pay a visit to a Vietnamese orphanage.

8

May 5, 1970

I went back to the O'Club at 1155 and waited at the door to the restaurant. After a few minutes, Happy emerged. He had changed from his waiter's smock to a short sleeve white shirt. He broke out into a broad smile when he saw me.

“I'm going to go back to the orphanage with you,” I said, “I want to see where you live.”

He smiled and grabbed hold of my hand. We walked the short distance to the main gate, and then he flagged down a motorized *xichlo mai*, which the GIs called a cyclo. I could see that this kid had street smarts well ahead of his age.

We were seated on a rickety seat in the front of the cyclo, a large tricycle, with the single wheel in the rear, powered by what sounded and smelled like a lawnmower engine. It took quite a while for the vehicle to reach the speed of the surrounding traffic, and the driver wasn't about to lose his momentum by stopping at red lights. We sailed through an intersection that was manned by a pith-helmeted member of the White Mice, the local police, who blew a shrill whistle as we passed. At another intersection, we barely missed an old Chevrolet sedan, but our driver was oblivious. It was clear to me our driver considered traffic lights as mere suggestions.

This was my first time off base in Vietnam, other than the short drives to the Freedom Hill BX and the marine base, Camp DaNang, on my previous tour in Vietnam. Unlike the off-base environment at DaNang, there were Americans everywhere in Saigon. The streets were crowded, and there were hawkers on every corner selling everything from flowers to fruit to souvenirs. On the few times we stopped at intersections, kids, probably no older than Happy, ran up to our cyclo, trying to reach inside my pockets. Happy yelled something at them in Vietnamese, and they scurried off.

We passed the well-guarded Presidential Palace, and about a mile afterward pulled up to a walled compound at the intersection of Cong Quynh and Vo Tanh streets. A hand-lettered sign read Hoi Duc Anh Orphanage.

I gave a few piasters to the driver and he yelled something at me. Happy yelled back, and the driver frowned and drove off.

Happy pointed to the main building, and said, “My house.”

I hadn't been sure what to expect, and I hoped my expression didn't reveal my disappointment. As we walked toward the main building, an army Sergeant carrying a large duffel bag walked out of the front door and, seeing me, saluted smartly.

“Are you here with the clothing drive from Ton Son Nhut, sir?”

“No, this is my first time here, and I wanted

to see where my young friend lives. We were together at the hospital at Cam Ranh."

"I remember when Chien arrived here from Cam Ranh. He had just gotten his glass eye, and he kept taking it out to show to everyone. The other kids really got a kick out of it."

It was the first time I had heard Happy's real name, Chien.

"What's his family name?" I asked.

"Le. His name's Chien Le."

"No," interrupted Happy, "My name Happy."

"Okay," the Sergeant said, "We want you to be happy, Happy."

"Have you been coming here long?" I asked.

"My unit, the First Signal Brigade Communications Site at Phu Lam, has been helping out here for over a year. We try to get our relatives in the States to donate supplies, clothing, toys, anything they can send our way. These kids need a lot of everything."

"Can you give me some contact information?" I asked, "I'm TDY here from Yokota, and I'll try to get a donation site set up there."

"I thought you'd never ask, sir." The Sergeant reached into his shirt pocket, pulled out a business card and handed it to me. "That APO address goes right to our headquarters. We can take it from there."

The Sergeant saluted again, said, "Good day, sir," and walked out of the compound.

"Okay, Happy, show me around."

Happy grabbed my hand again and took me from building to building.

There were kids everywhere. I could see that there were many more children than there were beds. In one room, with younger children, infants really, four children were lying sideways on one bed. There were a few cribs with rusty slats, and the sheets on all of the beds looked dirty. Actually, filthy.

"Washing machine is broken."

I turned around to see who had been reading my mind. The young nun appeared to be Eurasian, probably Vietnamese-French. She had virtually no accent.

"Sergeant Truman took a load of sheets to the base to get them laundered there. I'm Sister Theresa," she said, holding out her hand.

"I'm Hamilton Hancock," I responded, shaking her hand. "Chien and I are old friends from our time at the hospital at Cam Ranh."

"I've heard so much about you" she said, looking into my eyes. She grabbed my hand again in both of hers. "Please, keep calling him Happy. It's all he talks about."

"Have you been able to locate any of his relatives?" I asked.

She shook her head.

"We're his family now. He works at the base in the morning, then he takes care of the younger children in the afternoon. He calls them his new brothers and sisters. In fact, it's time for him to help with the infants. Do you want to lend a hand?"

"Sure. But I can only stay for a few hours. I have to fly out tonight."

We went into the infant ward and spent the next several hours changing diapers, giving baths, and feeding babies. Happy handled it like an old pro. It was the first time I'd ever done anything like that. It was really rewarding. Then it was time for me to return to the base.

I knelt down to look Happy in the eye, face-to-face.

"Happy, I have to go now, but I'll try to get back here as often as I can."

He grabbed my hand and walked me to the front gate. Then he gave me a long hug. I hugged back, then flagged down a cyclo. I looked forward to coming back soon.

9

May 6, 1970

We took off shortly after midnight. Our run was to DaNang to take a plane load of Colonels to a meeting, then we flew from DaNang to Ubon to carry imagery for photo-analysis. After a short layover at Ubon, we flew a repositioning flight to NKP, arriving at 0700. Another crew would be picking up the airplane to fly the reverse route.

We had 24 hours off. After we got a room at the VOQ, I walked over to the Jolly Green hootch. I knew Vince had already DEROSed, but thought I might recognize some of the guys I had met last year. A Captain saw me wandering around.

"Can I help you?"

"I was a friend of Jolly 22, Vince, and I was just looking around to see if there is anyone here I recognize."

“Friend of Vince?” He squinted and looked at my name tag. “Are you the famous Hamfist?”

“Guilty as charged.”

“Wow. It's a real pleasure to meet you. I've heard a lot about you.”

“I suspect it's mostly bullshit.”

“I'm Charlie North. I got here about a month before Vince DEROSed.”

“Pleased to meet you, Charlie. Do you know what kind of assignment Vince got?”

“He got an assignment to fixed-wing school with a follow-on assignment to a front-seat F-4. Most of us get assignments for stateside rescue units, but Vince had a lot of really high-visibility rescues, including yours. He was told he could pretty much write his own ticket.”

“That's great! Any idea where he's going in F-4s?”

“Not really. He didn't know his final base

assignment when he left here. He was totally pumped to go fixed-wing. I don't think he really cared where he would go."

I was getting hungry. It was breakfast time.

"Jeet jet, Charlie?

"No. Jew?"

That was a pilot-speak inside joke. What I was saying was, "Did you eat yet, Charlie?" and his response was, "No. Did you?"

"Where's the best place to get breakfast?" I asked.

"Follow me."

We went to the O'Club and had a great breakfast and a great conversation, and I really got to like Charlie. It dawned on me that it wasn't just Vince. *All* of the Jolly Green drivers I had met were really a special breed.

10

June 7, 1970

I was finally back at Yokota. This TDY had seemed to last a long time, although it had only been a little over three months. I was enjoying the flying, and feeling a real sense of accomplishment, doing an important job, but I missed Sam terribly when I was away.

I wished I hadn't made a commitment to Tom to wait a full year of engagement before we got married. I wanted to cement our relationship, make it something permanent. Something recognized and sanctified.

I had to admit, though, that going to pre-marital counseling had been really helpful. Our marriage would be stronger for having gone. I just wished we could start the marriage sooner.

This date marked three years since my graduation from the Academy. A lot had transpired during the intervening three years.

I'd been to pilot training. I'd been to combat. I'd lost friends, too many friends. And I'd finally been commissioned long enough to be promoted to Captain.

When I was in Vietnam, I served with numerous guys who had been required to wait five years or more to make Captain. When the waiting period to Captain was lowered to three years, around the time I graduated from the Academy, there was a lot of resentment among the guys who had waited longer. By now, there was just tacit acceptance.

This was a special date for me for another reason. I had been advised a week earlier to report to the Fifth Air Force Commander's office in my dress blue uniform at 0900 on June 7th. I asked Sam if she knew what it was all about, and she just smiled.

"You'll see," she said, "But I suggest you get a haircut."

I sent my uniform to the dry cleaner, and

when I picked it up I carefully put my new Captain bars on the shoulders – this would be the first day I would officially be a Captain – and put my wings and ribbons above the left pocket. Sam helped me arrange the ribbons in the proper order, carefully checking Air Force Regulation 35-10 to make sure they were correct. I was starting to get a pretty nice selection of "fruit salad" for someone with only three years of service.

I went to Fifth Air Force Headquarters at 0830, and walked up to Sam's desk at the Judge Advocate General Office. Sam's face lit up when she saw me. We stood around and made small talk for a few minutes, then she accompanied me to the Fifth Air Force Commander's office.

Nancy, the General's secretary, looked up and recognized Sam.

"Good morning, Captain Marcos." Then she looked at me. "You must be Captain Hancock!"

To be honest, it kind of caught me off guard being called Captain. I'd been "Lieutenant" for the past three years, and when I heard "Captain" I felt like looking behind me to see who Nancy was talking to.

"Pleased to meet you, Nancy, I'm Hamilton Hancock."

"It's a real pleasure to meet you, sir," she responded.

The telephone on the desk rang.

"Excuse me," Nancy said, picking up the phone. After a short pause, she answered, "Right away, General."

She turned to me.

"Please come with me, Captain Hancock." She looked at Sam, "You too, Captain Marcos."

We followed Nancy to a large briefing room. There was a long table with about twenty chairs around it, and about thirty chairs lined the walls. There was an officer, most of them Field

Grade, in every chair. There was a slightly raised stage at the far end of the room. The Fifth Air Force Commander, Lieutenant General "Wild Bill" Cody, was standing on the stage, along with his aide and a staff photographer.

Nancy escorted me up to the stage. Sam held back, standing against the wall. I wasn't sure what I should do, but I knew one thing for sure: when you meet a General, you salute.

The General returned my salute, then the aide spoke in a loud voice.

"Room, atten-hut!"

Everyone stood snapped to attention.

The aide opened a blue folder and withdrew a very formal-looking document, a certificate.

"Attention to orders.

The President of the United States of America, authorized by Title 10, Section 8742, United States Code, takes pleasure in presenting the Air Force Cross to Captain Hamilton H. Hancock, United States Air Force, for extraordinary heroism in military operations against an opposing armed force as a Forward Air Controller of the 20th Tactical Air Support Squadron, DaNang Air Base, Vietnam, in action at Chavane, Laos, on 21 December, 1969. On that day, Captain Hancock conducted an airstrike as a Forward Air Controller and then effected the rescue of a downed aircrew member under extremely hostile conditions in his lightly-armed O-2A aircraft. Using all tactical air support available, and finally his own aircraft ordnance, Captain Hancock, in desperation, disregarding extremely intense and accurate anti-aircraft fire, made repeated devastating low level attacks which stopped the hostile advance short of capturing the downed pilot. Captain Hancock then landed his heavily damaged aircraft in hostile territory to rescue the downed pilot. Captain Hancock's achievements were recognized by the Pacific Air Force

Commander as having personally saved the senior Air Force officer. Through his extraordinary heroism, superb airmanship, and aggressiveness in the face of the enemy, Captain Hancock reflected the highest credit upon himself and the United States Air Force."

As General Cody pinned the medal on my chest, the photographer was snapping one picture after another with his motorized Nikon. Out of the corner of my eye, I could see tears streaming down Sam's face. They had taught her well at Officer Training School – she remained at attention the whole time.

Then General Cody saluted me. After I returned his salute, he held out his hand.

"Congratulations, Hamilton," he said with a smile. "Or should I call you Hamfist?"

"Either name, General. Thank you, sir."

The General turned to the audience.

"At ease, lady, gentlemen. We have some

cake and drinks over here," he gestured toward the left front of the room, "and I'd like each of you to meet the recipient of the Air Force Cross, the second highest medal that can be given, second only to the Medal of Honor."

Sam and I went over to the table, and I stood there as a line formed and everyone came up to me to introduce themselves and congratulate me.

It was a really great day.

11

August 30, 1970

I was back in Vietnam with the Scatback operation, not due to return back to Yokota until December 2nd. I had real mixed emotions about the constant TDY to Vietnam.

Financially, it was a really good deal. I was getting TDY pay, combat pay and tax exemption. BX prices were much better than prices at the Yokota Exchange. And the cost of living was negligible.

But I really hated being away from home this much without even getting credit for another remote tour. The way the personnel system worked was that, if you got 180 continuous days TDY to a remote location, like Vietnam, you would get credit for a remote tour. Since I was always going for 93, maybe 94 days at a time, I didn't get remote credit, even though I exceeded 180 TDY days in a year.

When I would get back to Yokota I would have a couple of days off, then fly out on 2 or 3-day missions, usually to Korea or Okinawa. And just when I was finally getting used to being home, it would be time to deploy again. And all the time, I just couldn't wait to get back to Sam. I was starting to see the reality in the expression, "If the Air Force wanted you to have a wife, they would have issued one to you."

But I was doing what I had asked to do. Just because it didn't turn out to be what I had expected was nobody's fault but mine.

I would just have to learn to suck it up.

12

December 25, 1970

Christmas was an important date for me. It was the day I had left for Vietnam on my first tour. And the day I had met Tom, Samantha's father. And, of course, it was the day I had proposed to Sam.

So it was natural that we should be married on Christmas day. My mother had flown in a week earlier with Phil, my dad's war buddy. Mom was staying with Tom and Miyako, and Phil stayed at the Sanno, a military officer hotel in Akasaka.

Although Sam and I were each billeted in BOQ rooms, we had already been assigned an apartment in the new high-rise base housing apartment complex on the east side of the base. Sam was really effective at getting things done, and she somehow got us our keys two weeks early, so we were able to take our time moving all of our clothing, plus the small furniture items we each had, into the apartment. The Housing Supply Office provided the rest of the furniture we needed to turn the apartment into a real home.

Tom and Miyako had planned every aspect of the wedding. Mom wanted to help out, but by the time she had arrived in Japan, there was very little left to do.

We had a ceremony at the Base Chapel with about a hundred guests in attendance, then we had another, smaller, ceremony in the Shinto temple in downtown Fussa. It wasn't really a religious ceremony, more a formality to acknowledge Sam's heritage.

While Sam wore a long white wedding dress to the ceremony in the Chapel, she wore a beautiful kimono for the downtown event. Then she wore a white silk cocktail dress to the reception at the Officer's Club. She looked gorgeous in every outfit.

When the reception was nearing its end, we said our goodbyes to our guests and headed to the limousine that would drive us to the Haneda Hilton. We would be leaving from Haneda early the next morning for our honeymoon in Tahiti.

The guests were gathered around, throwing rice at us, and Tom, Miyako and my mom were waiting by the limousine door to be the last to send us off. We gave big hugs all around, got into the limo and drove off to start our life together.

13

February 28, 1971

Our honeymoon had been short, way too short. We should have stayed in Tahiti at least another week, but we were only able to get two weeks of leave for Sam.

It was tough going back to work. I had asked to be assigned a few 2-day or 3-day trips in theater, but I was needed back in Vietnam for another 3-month deployment to Scatback at the end of the month. This constant TDY was really starting to grate on me.

I started my TDY assignment at Yokota, carrying a 4-star General from Yokota Air Base to Kadena Air Base. Then we would reposition to Clark Air Base, to begin our Southeast Asia sequence.

I was paired up with Lieutenant Colonel Byers. When I saw his name on the schedule, I suspected I might have been getting a no-

notice check ride. In a roundabout way, I was.

During our mission briefing, Lieutenant Colonel Byers told me he wanted me to meet the General at planeside and provide the inflight briefing. And, he wanted me to fly the aircraft from the right seat. I didn't really understand his reasons, but, as Tennyson said in the poem, “ours not to reason why”.

I performed the preflight inspection and made sure that the baggage was stowed properly and the four-star placard was positioned in the left side cockpit window. The General's aide had arranged for baggage delivery ahead of time. Then, just before departure time, I stood at Parade Rest by the aircraft steps, on the left side of the aircraft. At exactly departure time, a staff car with a four-star flag on the antenna pulled up to planeside. I snapped to attention and gave my best Academy salute as the General approached the aircraft. He returned my salute and climbed the entry steps.

Lieutenant Colonel Byers was watching, and he started the right engine precisely as the General set foot on the steps. The General's aide followed, along with a Major, and I entered the airplane behind them and closed and locked the aircraft door as the left engine started.

As soon as I got strapped into my seat, Byers said, "Your airplane," and called for taxi clearance. We were pulling out of our parking spot less than 45 seconds after the General's staff car pulled up. Having a Code on board meant we got expeditious handling, and we were cleared for takeoff before we even reached the runway Hold Line.

I have to admit, my takeoff and climb-out were flawless. I had a General to impress, not to mention a Lieutenant Colonel who was probably evaluating me. After we reached cruise altitude, Flight Level 350, I made sure the plane was fully trimmed, then asked Lieutenant Colonel Byers if he wanted me to go back and brief the General.

"Good idea," he said, "but I'm telling you right now, I'm not going to touch the controls, so I hope you have it trimmed properly."

"In that case, sir, I need to give it a click of nose-down trim, since the CG will move a bit when I go aft."

He smiled. He knew I was right. The T-39 Sabreliner was so touchy in trim that the Center of Gravity would noticeably change when a pilot – or passenger – walked the short length of the interior. And the T-39 had no autopilot.

"You have the airplane," I said.

"Roger, I have the airplane."

It was time for me to brief the General and, in the vernacular of the T-39 pilot group, to play "ball-bearing stewardess", providing drinks and snacks to the passengers.

"Good morning, General. I'm Captain

Hancock. Our flight papers specify a 1035 local arrival at Kadena. Do you have any amendments or changes to our arrival time?"

It was critically important that we arrive exactly on time. When a General was scheduled to arrive at a base, there was usually a large reception party waiting on the ramp. Typically, it would be the Wing Commander, the Base Commander, plus any other Colonels and other high-ranking officers that were deemed appropriate. At Kadena, the Wing Commander was a one-star General. If we were late, there would be hell to pay for keeping the arrival party waiting. And if we were early and arrived before the reception party was in place, it would *really* be bad.

The General looked inquisitively at his aide, who shuffled through a file folder. The aide found what he was looking for.

"Ten thirty-five is still good, General," he said.

"Let's keep 1035, Captain."

"Yes, sir. General, would you care for any coffee or juice, or anything to eat? We have donuts and sandwiches." I paused for effect. "And we also have Orange Crush."

When he heard Orange Crush, the General's face lit up. I had learned from the VIP Briefing Sheet that the General was a diehard fan of the Denver Broncos, nicknamed the "Orange Crush". As a result, he absolutely loved Orange Crush soda. I had read the Briefing Sheet the previous night, and had gone to the BX and bought a large bottle of Orange Crush. The General was impressed.

I served Orange Crush to the General, and coffee and juice to the aide and the Major. No one wanted anything to eat. Apparently, they had attended some form of working breakfast. That meant Lieutenant Colonel Byers and I would have something to eat after the General deplaned at Kadena. Good deal.

I returned to my seat and resumed control of the aircraft. Our route of flight took us down the center of Japan, then south following the Ryukyu chain of islands to Okinawa. We were flying along airways, designated by VOR navigation stations that had Distance Measuring Equipment. I performed a DME groundspeed check from the Kagoshima VOR and compared it to our flight plan. We were making good time. Too good. We would be at least 13 minutes early at Kadena if we kept this speed. I took out my E6-B flight computer, which was really just a fancy circular slide rule with special aviation scales. I performed a quick calculation, and looked over at Lieutenant Colonel Byers.

"Sir, we need to slow to .74 Mach to arrive on schedule."

"Okay, Captain, you're flying. Make it happen."

I adjusted the throttles to reduce the fuel

flow by 200 pounds per hour, and after a few minutes the jet stabilized at .74. I saw a hint of a smile on Lieutenant Colonel Byers's face.

I performed groundspeed checks all the way down to Kadena. As we got closer, just prior to descent, I tuned the HF radio to WWV to get a time hack, and adjusted and set the aircraft clock. As we got close to the descent point, Lieutenant Colonel Byers started coughing.

"I'm having a hard time talking," he said, in a raspy voice. "You handle the radios also."

"Okay, no problem, sir."

If I was able to listen and talk on three radios while controlling an airstrike, I could sure as hell fly and talk on just one radio at the same time.

Naha Center transferred me to Kadena Approach Control, and I advised them we had a Code on board and needed to touch down at 1032 local. That would give me 3 minutes to taxi to Base Ops, the parking location for high-ranking passengers.

It was a crystal clear morning as we descended over Okinawa. I marveled at the beautiful turquoise ocean and white sand beaches. The beaches were outstanding, and, I had to admit, the ocean was even more beautiful than the Gulf, near my home in Pensacola. I checked the time, and it looked like we might have been about a minute ahead of schedule. I decided to configure early, and lowered approach flaps.

"Kadena Air Base 12 o'clock, seven miles. Report airport in sight," instructed the Approach Controller.

"Airport in sight," I responded. I glanced over at Lieutenant Colonel Byers. He hadn't done a thing the whole flight.

"Are you okay, boss?" I asked.

He nodded.

"Contact Tower," instructed Approach.

"Roger." Pause. "Good day." I always tried to give a short pause and say "Good day" the way Paul Harvey did.

"Kadena Tower, Scatback 403, gear down, final."

"Scatback 403, wind 040 at 7, cleared to land, runway 5 Right."

I looked at the aircraft clock. It was 1031 local.

I put down final flaps, and touched down at exactly 1032. I made the high-speed turnoff, and taxied toward the parking spot. With about 100 yards to go, we were still about a minute early, so I slowed down a bit.

As we turned to park, I shut down the left engine, and coasted to a stop with the red carpet lined up abeam the aircraft door. I set the parking brake, shut down the right engine and checked the clock. It was 1034 and 50 seconds. I hopped out of my seat and opened the door for the general.

He stepped out onto the tarmac at 1035.

To the second.

14

February 28, 1971

After the General and his party deplaned, Lieutenant Colonel Byers looked at me.

"Any sandwiches left over? I'm starved."

His voice had miraculously cleared up.

"I'm sure you are, sir. You must have worked up quite an appetite on the way down here." As soon as I said it, I was afraid I had overstepped my bounds.

"Actually, I did," he responded. "Do you know how hard it is to pay total attention to everything and act like you're out to lunch?"

I had a puzzled look on my face.

"I just gave you your IP readiness evaluation, and you did great. We'll do some more IP training on the way down to Clark, and then I'll designate you as an IP."

"Sir, I'm flattered, but I've never done any instructing."

"You're going to practice instructing me all the way down to Clark. At first, it will be difficult, but you'll get the hang of it. You already know how to talk and fly. Mostly, I want you to be an IP because we have a lot of Generals who want to get stick time, and they have to have an IP in the right seat whenever they fly the Sabreliner. When you fly with a General, you're pretty much flying solo, just like you were on the way here."

I was looking forward to the challenge.

15

March 23, 1971

I'd been flying throughout Southeast Asia pretty much nonstop since arriving at the end of February. Every now and then I got 24 hours off in Saigon, and got a chance to visit Happy and deliver supplies to the orphanage.

Like everything she tackled, Sam had done an incredible job collecting donations for the orphanage. She got sheets, blankets, pillows, food, toys, all the things they needed. And then she used her feminine wiles to convince transient T-39 crews to take the supplies to Saigon, where they were held for me at Base Ops. And then I'd take them to the orphanage.

Every time I went through Base Ops in Saïgon, I looked for the packages. They were always there. And there would always be a "care package" for me, too. Cookies, a small cake, or perhaps my favorite, what I called a

"Japanese hamburger".

It wasn't really a hamburger, it just looked like one. It was actually a dessert called *dorayaki*, made of two small pancakes sandwiching sweet azuki bean paste. It was delicious. I loved it, and it was only available in Japan. And Sam always managed to include several in a package to me, along with a note telling me how much she loved, and missed, me.

This was a night flight to Ton Son Nhut Air Base, in Saigon, from DaNang. We were on final approach right at midnight when the city came under rocket attack. Ton Son Nhut Tower sent us around, and we performed a missed approach and circled over the city until things calmed down, about fifteen minutes. The base itself hadn't been hit, and once the runway was inspected, we were cleared to land.

We secured the airplane and went to the BOQ. As we checked in at the Billeting Office, several of the Vietnamese clerks were staring at me and talking among themselves. I checked my reflection in the window of the entry door, to see if I looked funny. Maybe a cut or a scratch. I looked okay. I couldn't figure out why they were staring.

Finally, one of the clerks, a young girl, came up to me.

“You *Dai Uy* Hamcox, yes?”

Dai Uy was the Vietnamese word for Captain.

“Yes, Hancock,” I answered. “What can I do for you?”

“Rocket hit Hoi Duc Anh Orphanage. You friend, he live there, yes?”

I dropped my bags and ran toward the door before she had even finished speaking. I needed to get to the orphanage, and fast. I ran all the way to the main gate, then flagged down a cyclo. I shouted “Go, go, go” at every intersection. Fuck the red lights.

As we approached the orphanage, there was rubble all over the street. There were firemen putting out the remains of a blaze in what was left of a government building. The smell of burning buildings, and death, hung in the air.

We pulled up to the orphanage main entrance, or, rather, what had been the main entrance. Now it was just a pile of bricks. I threw all of my *piasters* to the driver and ran inside.

“Happy! Happy! Where are you? Happy!” I bellowed.

No answer.

I saw a nun, not Sister Theresa, a nun I hadn't seen before.

“I'm looking for Chien.”

She had a blank look on her face. I think she was in shock.

“Chien Le. He has one eye. He calls himself Happy.”

I heard a voice behind me.

“I'm so sorry, Captain.”

I turned to see Sister Theresa. She had tears streaming down her face. She came up and hugged me, sobbing uncontrollably.

“I'm so sorry,” she wept, “Happy has passed away.”

16

March 25, 1971

The past two days had been a blur. After I left the orphanage, I called the Scatback Ops Officer and asked for an extra day off in Saigon. He gave it to me without even asking me why.

I was the only one like a family Chien had. I told Sister Theresa I wanted to perform the burial ritual.

"Are you sure you want to do this?" she asked. "His body is really in bad shape."

"It's my duty. I'm his only family."

I had been given instructions from the Mortuary Affairs Office. I washed his small body, placed a chopstick between his teeth and put several grains of rice and three coins in his mouth, and wrapped his body in white cloth. Then I put his body in the diminutive coffin, and helped lower it into the grave.

"Goodbye, Happy. Go in peace, join your parents and your brother Grumpy. I'll help your country. And I'll get even. I promise."

17

March 25, 1971

I desperately wished I could see Happy one last time. I already missed him. The way his face lit up when he saw me. The way he held my hand when he took me around the orphanage, to show me how he had passed out the supplies I had brought. The way he cleaned his glass eye by popping it into his mouth like a big gum ball.

I wanted to cry, but I couldn't. I had seen too much death, lost too many friends, to grieve. Now I was wracked by uncontrollable, overpowering rage. I had seen enough. I wanted to get even. I wanted to do whatever it took to stop those fuckers from bringing rockets down from Hanoi to rain death and destruction on innocent civilians.

I knew I was helping the war effort by carrying Generals, and Ambassadors, and supplies, and photographic imagery, all over Southeast Asia in my T-39.

But now I needed to do more. I needed to get back into interdiction. I needed to bring the war to those bastards doing this destruction. I needed to bomb them back to the fucking stone age.

I needed to get into a fighter.

18

April 3, 1971

I was back flying. It was where I needed to be. When I was flying, I could compartmentalize, I could forget my problems. I could concentrate on getting the job done, accomplishing the mission. I would be heading back to Yokota soon, and I actually wanted to fly right now.

This day we would be carrying a two-star from Ubon to Saigon. An easy day flight. And the General, a late manifest addition, had advised Operations that he wanted to get some stick time, so I was assigned to be the IP in the right seat.

I supervised the loading of the aircraft, and then got into the right seat and told my copilot, Captain Nick Nicholson, to stand by the door to greet the General, and invite him to the left seat of the cockpit. I heard the General's staff car arrive, and I pressed the starter for the right engine as I heard his foot hit the aircraft steps.

The General entered the cramped cockpit and sat down in the left seat.

"Welcome aboard, General," I said. "I'm Captain..." I paused in mid-sentence, as I looked at my passenger. He was looking back at me, his mouth open in shock.

It was former Brigadier General, now Major General, McCall, Sharkbait 41 Alpha, the pilot I had rescued in Laos!

I held out my hand, and he shook it and gave a half-assed attempt to give me a hug. The cockpit was too small, and I was already strapped into my seat, so he settled for putting his arm around my shoulders and giving a big squeeze.

"Hamfist! I was hoping I'd run into you one of these days!"

"Congratulations on your promotion,

General."

"Thanks. You too, Hamfist. But my promotion wouldn't have been possible without you."

It was time to start engines, and we were both all business as we taxied out, took off, and climbed to altitude. Once we were in cruise phase, we had time to talk.

"How are you enjoying the T-39?"

"It's a great airplane, General, and I really appreciate your help in getting me this assignment. But..."

I paused. I didn't want to seem like an ingrate.

"What is it, Hamfist?"

"Well, General, I had asked for the assignment because my girlfriend, who's now my wife, was based at Yokota. But, to be honest, I'm not seeing her very much. I'm TDY to the Scatback operation almost all the time.

And if I'm going to be gone, and in Vietnam anyway..."

"You want a fighter, right?" he interrupted.

I nodded.

"Hamfist, I'll get you whatever you want. If you want a fighter to the States, Europe, wherever, just tell me where. And I'll get your wife a joint spouse assignment to the same base."

"Thank you, General. Sir, you may think I'm crazy, but I want to come back to Vietnam."

Then I opened up to the General. I told him about Happy. I told him how I wanted to help the South Vietnamese stop this outrageous war. I wanted to go back over the trail, to do whatever I could to stop them from bringing rockets down from the north. I told him I wanted vengeance.

"Hamfist, I'm going to get you your fighter to Vietnam. But I want you to rethink your motives. If all you want to do is get even, it will be a hollow victory every time you pickle off your bombs."

"When you were killing those gomers at Chavane," he continued, "you weren't doing it to get even with them for shooting me down. You were doing it to save my ass. Sooner or later, we're going to start a bombing campaign over North Vietnam again. When you drop your bombs on Hanoi, I want it to be because you want to stop the flow of munitions to the south, to end the war, not because you want revenge. If all you do is bomb them to get even, you'll be no different than the bastards who blew up the orphanage."

I felt like I had just awakened from an endless nightmare.

"You're right, sir. Thank you."

The General's words had really opened my eyes and helped me get my head on straight.

And finally, I was able to cry for Happy.

19

June 17, 1971

I had been waiting for the call for several weeks, and it came in the morning. The phone in our on-base quarters at Yokota rang at 0800. I had slept in late, since I didn't have to brief for my flight until 1100.

"Hello. This is Captain Hancock."

"Captain Hancock, this is Captain Myers, at the Military Personnel Center. I have your pipeline SEA assignment for you."

"Excellent. What do you have for me?"

"We have a front seat F-4 for you. But I want to confirm that you are a volunteer for a second SEA tour. This is pipeline Southeast Asia. It won't be an F-4 to Europe or stateside."

"That's affirmative, Captain. I am a volunteer for a second tour in Southeast Asia."

"Okay, we have your fighter lead-in course

scheduled for July 7th, at Myrtle Beach Air Force Base. Then we have water survival scheduled for July 24th at Homestead. We have several options for your RTU. We can keep you at Homestead, or send you to MacDill Air Force Base or Luke Air Force Base. Your choice."

The F-4 RTU – Replacement Training Unit – training would last about six months, so it was pretty important to get a base assignment I would enjoy. I didn't really know much about any of the bases, but I did know that Homestead was near Miami. I'd been to Miami Beach when I was a kid. The beaches weren't as nice as the beaches near my home, at Pensacola, but the night life was a lot better. Great restaurants and activities. Okay, I would go for Miami.

"I'll take Homestead."

"You've got it, Captain. Fighter lead-in at Myrtle Beach, the rest of your training at Homestead. You'll have your orders by this time tomorrow."

"Thank you, Captain Myers."

"You're welcome, Captain Hancock. Good luck."

It wasn't until after I hung up that I realized that Captain Myers at MPC had been working late. A call at 0800 in Japan worked out to 1800 local time – 6:00 p.m. – at MPC Headquarters in San Antonio, Texas. Nice to know the Personnel people kept working until the job was done. Maybe Fish, my former room-mate in Vietnam, had been a little rough on them in his assessment.

I walked into the kitchen. Sam had already left for work, and had cooked my breakfast and left it in the Amana Radarange. The Amana was one of the first appliances we bought when we got married. We got it at the Pony Store, right off base, the same week we returned from our honeymoon. It was really a godsend. I didn't know how people got along without one.

I showered and shaved, put on my uniform and headed out the door early. I needed to tell Sam about my assignment, and I didn't want to be rushed.

20

June 17, 1971

I entered the Fifth Air Force Judge Advocate General Office and walked over to Sam's desk.

"Good morning, Captain Hancock," I said.

"Good morning, Captain Hancock," she smiled.

I really wanted to give her a good-morning kiss, but I held back.

We always got a kick about scrupulously avoiding Public Display of Affection and putting on an act of formality whenever we were in uniform. We knew that nobody would really mind a little PDA from newlyweds, but we wanted to keep our behavior strictly professional when we were at work. And it heightened our passion once we were finally alone.

"Can you take a little time off for a cup of

coffee?"

Sam looked at her desk calendar, checked her watch, and nodded.

"I need to be on a conference call at ten," she said.

I looked at my Rolex.

"No problem," I responded, "I just want to chat with you for a few minutes. Let's take my car. I'm parked in the General's spot."

Sam started to respond, then broke out into a broad smile. She knew me well enough to know I wouldn't be *that* stupid.

We drove to the Officer's Club and went to the casual bar, called The Outback. I ordered two coffees and locked eyes with Sam.

"Sam, I..."

"You got your fighter!" she interrupted. "I can see it in your face."

Damn, she was sharp! I'd better never try to

keep a secret from her.

“Ham, I'm so happy for you! And I've been in the airplane when you were flying, so I know what a great pilot you are. Of course I'll worry about you, and I'm going to miss you, just like I miss you when you are TDY. But you'll be doing what you love, and you'll be doing something incredibly important.”

“I love you, honey.”

“I love you, too,” she replied. She looked around. We were alone in The Outback. She leaned over and gave me a passionate kiss. “Now, let's get back to work.”

21

July 7, 1971

The flight from Yokota to Atlanta seemed to take forever. I was on a packed Northwest Orient Boeing 747 military charter flight that stopped at Anchorage, Alaska for a fuel stop, then continued on to Atlanta.

The Yokota Traffic Management Office, which handled my transportation arrangements, advised me that I would be reimbursed for a rental car to drive to Myrtle Beach Air Force Base, in South Carolina. I opted for a Mustang – nobody said I had to rent a Chevy Nova!

Myrtle Beach was home to the 354th Tactical Fighter Wing. The wing consisted of an operational A-7 fighter squadron and the Tactical Air Command Fighter lead-in School. In a brief two-week period, I would learn fundamental Air Combat Maneuvers – ACM –

and gunnery in an AT-33.

The AT-33 “Shooting Star”, nicknamed the “T-Bird” was basically a T-33 trainer aircraft fitted with a basic gun sight, a .50 caliber machine gun, a bomb rack under the fuselage, and hard points under the wings for rocket pods. The aircraft itself was old, really old. The T-33 had made its maiden flight in 1948, and was a derivative of the Lockheed P-80 “Shooting Star”, the first American jet fighter aircraft.

The T-33 had been used for Undergraduate Pilot Training – UPT – until the mid-1960s. After it was replaced by the T-37 and T-38 at UPT, it was pretty much sidelined and used for proficiency flying and support roles at various Air Force bases around the world. I was actually looking forward to flying the AT-33, since I had heard the “old head” Instructor Pilots at UPT talking about flying the T-Bird, and it was going to be pretty neat to fly an antique airplane.

I drove very carefully for the six-hour trip to Myrtle Beach, since I had been driving on the left side of the road for the past year and a half. I had to really concentrate at every intersection, to make sure I stayed on the proper side.

I checked in at the Visiting Officer Quarters, then went to the 354th Headquarters, and was directed to the "schoolhouse". At the Training Squadron I met up with the 13 other pilots who became my classmates. About half of the guys had flown O-2s, and the rest were Lieutenants right out of UPT. One of the first things we did after checking in at the Training Squadron was report to the Life Support Section.

At Life Support, the Staff Sergeant wanted each of us to sit in an ejection seat mock-up to see if we would fit into the cockpit. The geometry of the T-33 cockpit presented problems for taller pilots. One of the guys in the class, Spike Spiker, was a tall, lanky Lieutenant right out of UPT.

“Lieutenant,” the Staff Sergeant said, “if you have to bail out of the T-33, there's a good chance you're going to lose your knees.”

That certainly got everyone's attention. The Staff Sergeant looked each of us over.

“I need everyone to go through our anthropomorphic mock-up, to see if you can eject safely.”

In the center of the room there was an ejection seat, and a rail with a sliding metal form in the shape of a canopy bow, the top of the aircraft windscreen. The metal form represented the front part of the aircraft canopy that remained during an ejection sequence.

“When you start the ejection by raising these handles,” the Staff Sergeant said, “the canopy will separate. Then this initiator will fire and the seat will move up the rails. This,” he was pointing at the metal form, “represents the canopy bow. Let's see if it clears Lieutenant

Spiker's knees."

Spike sat in the seat and the Staff Sergeant carefully lowered the metal form down the rail. It hit his kneecaps.

"I'm sorry, Lieutenant, but you don't qualify to fly the T-33. If you need to eject, you'll lose your legs."

Spike looked devastated.

"Don't worry, Lieutenant, you'll still attend ground school, and you'll get a few additional training sorties when you go to RTU."

The whole reason for fighter lead-in was to get the basics out of the way in an aircraft with lower operating cost than our final fighters. So Spike would get his fighter lead-in training in his real fighter. Not a problem, especially since he was coming right out of UPT and had recent formation flying experience.

Spike was the only guy in our class with long legs, so the rest of us were okay to fly the T-bird. But before we could fly, we needed ground school. A lot of ground school.

The rest of the day was devoted to getting our life support equipment fitted. Oxygen masks, CRU-60/P oxygen connectors, parachute harnesses, G-suits, helmets. We also received the T-33 Flight Manual, officially T.O. 1-T-33-1, called the “Dash one”, and several soft-cover books covering formation flying, gun sight calculations, ballistics, and Air Combat Maneuvering.

After we adjourned, I went by the O'Club for a quick snack, then retreated to my room to start hitting the books. There was a lot to learn, even with my experience in tactical operations. It must have been a really steep hill to climb for the guys right out of UPT.

After a few hours of reading about mill setting calculations and ballistic parameters, I was fast asleep.

It was a good thing I had set the alarm,

because we had a full day ahead of us.

22

July 8, 1971

Our training for the next two weeks would consist of academic instruction in the morning, then flying training in the afternoon.

There was a lot to learn. For starters, we got a quickie course in T-33 systems and procedures. The T-bird was a fairly simple airplane, but it wasn't easy to fly. It required the pilot to be well ahead of the airplane at all times, due to the slow throttle response.

The Allison J-33 engine in the T-33 took forever to accelerate. Specifically, it took 15 seconds to go from Idle power to full Military power. That meant you really need to anticipate power requirements, such as when a landing needed to be aborted. You could use up a lot of runway while waiting for the engine to accelerate to go-around power.

Speed-wise, the T-33 was pretty compatible

with the T-39 I'd been flying. In that regard I, along with my classmates right out of UPT, had an easier adjustment than the guys coming back after flying the O-2A.

When I had been flying the O-2A, I didn't know anything about gun sight geometry and munitions ballistics. I just knew to put the pipper on the target and squeeze off a rocket when everything looked correct. We called it the TLAR weapons release system – That Looks About Right.

For real weapons delivery, with a plethora of ordnance available, gun sight computations were critical. Every munition had a specific set of ballistic parameters, based on its weight, drag index, dive angle, airspeed and release altitude.

Complicating the calculation was the reality that, in a steep dive, the altimeter would lag the aircraft and indicate higher than the actual altitude. We had to calculate altimeter lag for each delivery, again based on dive angle, airspeed and altitude. And, of course, to do it absolutely perfectly, we would need to correct the altimeter error for non-standard temperature. We spent a good portion of every briefing for gunnery range missions doing our computations, but soon learned that the TLAR system worked in fighters, too.

Typically, on a bomb run at the gunnery range, we would initiate the delivery by rolling to a bank angle of 90 degrees plus the final dive angle. For a 30-degree delivery, that would be a 120-degree bank for the roll-in. The more standard 45-degree delivery would require a 135-degree bank for the roll-in.

When rolling out on the delivery heading, the depression of the gun sight, measured in "mills" – short for the geometric term "milliradians" – would cause the pipper to swing left and right during every heading correction. This swinging was called "pendulum effect". This pendulum effect made it essential to be steady on the run-in heading as quickly as possible, so the pipper would track correctly to the aim point.

The pipper had to track to the aim point, not the target. Unless the wind was calm, the aim point would be somewhere other than on the target. During delivery, the bomb would respond to the wind affecting the aircraft at the point of delivery. If there was a 30-knot wind at delivery altitude, the pilot would need to calculate an offset aim point upwind of the actual target, by an amount determined by the munitions ballistics. Typically, this offset aim point was a calculation that needed to be computed by the pilot during the roll-in for the delivery.

For me, math in public was always an embarrassing event. Computing an offset aim point while in a 135-degree bank, and at the same time calculating a weapons release altitude by considering the target elevation, was challenging. Really challenging.

On the weapons range, we learned about compensating errors. If the dive angle was shallower than planned, the bombs would land short of the target. If the angle was steeper than planned, the bombs would be long. If the G-loading on the airplane was not correct for the dive angle, the bombs would be either short or long. For example, in a 45-degree dive the airplane should have .707 Gs of loading. If loading was too heavy, the bombs would be short. If loading was too light, the bombs would be long.

Of course, airspeed dramatically affected the bomb delivery. Too slow, the bombs would be short, too fast, they'd be long.

The goal of every bomb run was to have the pipper exactly on the offset aim point at the precise point where the aircraft reached the delivery altitude, at exactly the correct G-loading and airspeed.

“Every year, somewhere in the world,” said

Major Joe Cooley, our academic instructor, "a pilot makes his parameters perfectly. The rest of the time, we compensate."

So, if we are steep and fast, we pickle a bit early. If we're slow or shallow, we press a bit and pickle a little late. TLAR.

Every mission, we flew in formation. I had gotten pretty rusty in my formation flying, since I hadn't done it for almost three years, but I got back into the swing of it pretty quickly.

Air Combat Maneuvering was an extension of formation flying. We didn't perform a lot of ACM during fighter lead-in, since the T-33 was a straight-wing airplane, and all of the modern fighters were swept-wing. A swept-wing operates a lot different from a straight wing at high angles of attack, which is pretty much the standard environment during an engagement. We'd get our real ACM training at RTU.

My biggest surprise on the gunnery range

was the strafe event, using the internal .50 caliber gun. All of the war movies I had seen as a kid had led me to believe that bullets should walk across the target during a strafing run. *Au contraire!* The goal is to get every bullet to go through the same hole. This required slight, very slight, forward pressure on the stick during the strafing run, since the distance to target rapidly decreases as the airplane closes to the target.

The fighter lead-in training was over in a heartbeat, and it was time for me to head down to Homestead Air Force Base for Water Survival, followed by F-4 RTU.

I found a 1964 Corvair for sale for $300 in the local paper, bought it for my journey, and returned the rental car. Corvairs were really cheap after publication of Nader's book, *Unsafe At Any Speed.* I bought a Sway-Bar from the J.C. Whitney catalog, installed it, and had a safe car for my time in the States.

23

July 25, 1971

Water Survival was a lot of fun, but at times a bit scary. We started out with a few days of class, learning about life rafts, individual flotation gear, signaling devices, and water purification. Then we covered hypothermia. Even in warm water, like we had off the coast of Florida, and Vietnam, it was possible to die from hyperthermia in fairly short order. Getting out of the water and into the life raft was essential.

The graduation exercise was the scary part. My mistake had been going to the movies while I was at Myrtle Beach. I had gone to see the new shark movie, *Blue Water, White Death*. Not a smart move, considering I would be out in the ocean a week later, out of sight of land, all by myself.

The dozen of us in the class boarded a

powerboat and headed out to the open ocean. We were each outfitted with a parachute harness and a hard-shell ejection seat survival kit attached by a lanyard. One by one, we had parachutes hooked up to our harnesses, and at the appropriate time we were towed aloft by the boat until we were approximately 300 feet in the air.

On signal, we would release the tow rope and descend to the water, as if we had just parachuted out of our aircraft. We were each deposited about a mile apart. After the boat released all of the students, it took off for shore.

The mission was to inflate the under-arm Life Preserver Units on the way down to the water, deploy and inflate the one-man life raft, climb aboard, then use whatever equipment we needed in the survival kit to effect our rescues. Included in the exercise was the requirement to use the water desalinization kit to produce potable water.

As soon as I hit the water, my parachute collapsed on top of me. I knew from training that there would be some disorientation, and it was comforting to be mentally prepared. As instructed, I grabbed the closest seam in the parachute canopy and followed it to the edge, to get out from under it.

The water was cold. Shockingly cold. The water was also incredibly clear. I could see down hundreds of feet, and, well below me, I saw menacing shapes moving around. I was motivated to get into the life raft as quickly as I could. Highly motivated.

One of the things I hadn't anticipated was the difficulty of getting aboard the life raft with the inflated LPUs under my arms. They really got in the way, and when I pushed them behind my arms they tended to push me face-down into the water. Eventually I got into the raft, deployed the sea anchor and the marking dye, and opened my survival kit.

The desalinization kit was easy to find. It was a rectangular metal can, similar in appearance to a Band-Aid box. It contained a powder which, when mixed with sea water, would produce drinkable, albeit unpleasant tasting, water. I opened the kit just as a large gust of wind hit my raft. The powder went flying all over, including into my eyes.

Now I had a real problem. I was temporarily blinded by the stinging powder in my eyes, and I couldn't see the contents of my survival kit to find the can of drinking water I would need to rinse out my eyes. I was starting to get really worried.

Then I thought about what I'd been through before, when there were real gomers shooting at me, and this didn't seem so bad. I would be uncomfortable for a little while, but eventually someone would spot my marker dye even if I didn't signal. No one was trying to kill me. This too would pass.

After what seemed like an eternity I found the can of drinking water, opened it and poured it all over my face and eyes. My eyes still burned, but my vision returned. I located the URC-64 transceiver radio in my survival vest and made contact with the pickup helicopter. When he requested for me to mark my spot, I popped a signal smoke. He lowered the hoist and I dutifully waited for it to touch the water to electrically ground it.

As they hoisted me into the HH-53, I had a momentary flashback to the last time I had come aboard a helicopter. Nobody was shooting at me now, I was off the coast of Miami, and the only problem I had was a little pink-eye. All's right with the world.

The PJ gave me the once-over as I came aboard.

"Are your eyes okay, sir?"

"Just a little salt water, Sarge. I'm fine."

I was safe, I was getting dry, I was

uninjured, and in two more days I'd be starting F-4 training.

Yeah, I was fine.

24

August 2, 1971

I had finished Water Survival school a few days earlier, and had the weekend off. F-4 RTU class started on Monday.

The F-4 Phantom II was a big airplane. Up until now, I'd been flying small planes. The O-2A weighed in at 4850 pounds max gross weight. The T-39 was approximately 10,000 pounds. In sharp contrast, the F-4 grossed out at 49,000 pounds. It was a giant, fire-breathing monster.

The original Air Force F-4C was an offspring of the Navy F-4B, an interceptor aircraft that flew off of aircraft carriers. Unlike previous fighters, it didn't have a gun. At the time of its development, the thinking was that missiles would replace guns during dogfights. For air-to-air combat, it carried missiles, the AIM-7 and the AIM-9.

The AIM-7 Sparrow was a radar-guided missile with a warhead that contained 88 pounds of high explosives. It was a big missile, 12 feet long, weighing over 500 pounds. To fire the AIM-7, you first had to lock onto the target with the aircraft radar, ensure that the target was in range, and fire. The missile would guide to the target only as long as you maintained a radar lock-on. It had a speed in excess of Mach 2, and cost roughly the price of a Rolls Royce automobile. An attack with an AIM-7 was referred to as a "Fox 1" attack.

The AIM-9 Sidewinder was an infra-red heat-seeking missile with a 20-pound warhead. It also had a speed in excess of Mach 2. It was smaller than the AIM-7, at 10 feet long and just under 200 pounds. Unlike the scenes in the movies, you needed to ensure that the IR seeker head saw the target before you fired it. The pilot would know the missile saw the target when he heard a steady tone in his headset. An AIM-9 attack was referred to as a "Fox 2".

The F-4 was capable of carrying another Fox 2 missile, the AIM-4 Falcon. It was a much smaller missile, and had a really small 7-pound warhead. It was produced by Hughes, and some pilots jokingly called it the "Hughes Arrow", because they said that the only way you could kill another aircraft with it was if you shot the pilot through the heart.

The Air Force F-4C and F-4D did not have an internal cannon, but were capable of carrying a centerline-mounted external M61 Vulcan Gatling gun. The F-4E had an internal nose-mounted Vulcan. The Vulcan was an incredible weapon, with a rate of fire in excess of 100 rounds per second from its six barrels. And every 20 millimeter round contained a high explosive warhead. The internal gun carried 640 rounds. A gun attack was called a "Fox 3".

During our time at the RTU, we were going to be trained, and theoretically become proficient, in all three methods of air-to-air attack. There was a fourth method of attack, called the Fox 4. The "Fox 4" maneuver was a last-ditch effort to down an enemy aircraft by ramming it. Needless to say, we never intentionally practiced the Fox 4 maneuver.

There were 20 of us in the class, ten formed crews composed of front-seat pilots and rated navigators as back-seat Weapons Systems Officers, WSOs. Most of the WSOs were young guys, right out of Navigator school.

All of us, the pilots, had performed airborne acrobatics routinely in pilot training. Not so for the navs. In fact, there was virtually nothing they learned in Navigator school, other than meteorology, that prepared them for the back seat of an F-4. It was a really steep hill for them to climb.

Fortunately, they were sharp, they were gung-ho, and they were young. God, they were young! My assigned WSO, Bob Diller, looked barely old enough to shave. Somehow, Bob had picked up the nickname Deacon.

Name-wise, I was still Hamilton, sometimes called Ham. It started to look like the moniker *Hamfist* was fading from memory.

Until the first day of ground school.

25

August 2, 1971

When I showed up at the RTU squadron, I processed in and went to the mass briefing room. On this first day of training we would all be addressed by the Wing Director of Operations. All 20 of us were in position about ten minutes early. Then, from the back of the room, I heard a yell, a voice from the past.

"Hamfist!"

I turned to see who had outed me. It was Captain Kane, from DaNang!

"Speedbrake!"

Damn, it was good to see him!

"I'm going to be your IP, Hamfist, so you'd better behave yourself."

"Damn, it's good to see you, Speedbrake. Have you been in F-4s all this time?"

"Yeah. After DaNang, I went to Spangdahlem for two years, became an IP over there, and just got to Homestead a few months ago. You're going to love this airplane."

"I'm really looking forward to flying it."

We were just starting to catch up with each other, when someone shouted, "Room, atten-hut!"

The DO had arrived. Colonel West was a big man with a shaved head and a stern look about him. A dead ringer for the actor Telly Savalas. When Colonel West talked, everyone listened.

"Gentlemen, welcome to Homestead. You're fortunate to be attending the best RTU in Tactical Air Command."

"I'll tell you why it's the best," he continued, "It's the best because we have the highest standards, and the highest wash-out rate, in TAC. We will demand the best you can give us, and for some of you, it just won't be good enough. But for those of you who graduate, you'll be some of the best new fighter pilots in the Air Force."

"Now before I tell you what I consider the most important quality of a fighter pilot, and this goes for you WSOs also, I'm going to tell you a story."

"During Operation Rolling Thunder, an F-105 flight lead was in an extended engagement with a MiG. He was performing repeated high-speed yoyos, gaining on the MiG with each yoyo. One more yoyo and he would be in a firing position."

The Colonel paused and looked around the room. We were all transfixed in rapt attention.

"Just as he was about to get a firing solution, his wingman called Bingo."

Bingo meant that the fuel had reached the predetermined quantity where the flight must Return To Base.

"What do you think Lead did?"

Colonel West made eye contact with each of us. I was hoping he wasn't expecting any of us to answer.

"Lead did what he was supposed to do," he continued, "he disengaged by doing a quarter roll and zoom, and he RTB'd. And I'll tell you why he did it. He did it because he had flight discipline. And he had trust. He trusted that his wingman wouldn't call Bingo unless he was really at Bingo fuel. And he, the Flight Lead, had established that Bingo. He gave up his MiG because he had discipline. If he had taken one more slice, done one more yoyo, he could have had that MiG. But he would have put his wingman in jeopardy. He did the right thing. He had discipline."

"I expect, I *demand*, that all my pilots exhibit discipline. I don't expect anyone to be perfect in his flying. You're going to make mistakes, and you're going to learn from your mistakes. But I do expect everyone to have perfect discipline. If anyone in the flight calls

Bingo, you RTB, whether you've accomplished your training or not. If anyone calls Knock It Off, you discontinue the maneuver. And if you find yourself out of control below 10,000 feet, you eject."

"Does anyone have any questions?"

Nobody uttered a word.

"Gentlemen, I wish you well in your training."

With that, the Colonel walked to the door. Someone shouted, "Room, atten-hut!" and we all snapped to attention as the Colonel exited.

There was no doubt in anyone's mind what our priorities would be.

26

August 2, 1971

We were all anxious to get into the airplanes and get flying. When we saw the training syllabus, we were shocked – we wouldn't be in the airplanes for weeks. The closest we would get was the simulator, and that wouldn't even happen for another two weeks.

We did get to go up close and personal to an F-4 early into our academics, when we were studying aircraft systems. After spending an hour teaching us about the Utility Hydraulic System, our instructor surprised us.

"Get your ear plugs and follow me. We're going outside. No hats."

We followed him to the flight line and waited. The flight line was the one place on base where hats were not worn, since they posed a serious FOD – Foreign Object Damage – hazard if they were ingested into engine intakes.

After a few minutes of waiting, we saw an F-4 taxi up near us, and then observed the Auxiliary Air Doors in operation. They were small doors in the belly of the airplane, and they opened up just as the airplane taxied to the parking area. It was unbelievably noisy with the engines running, and we could barely hear what the instructor was saying.

"The Aux Air Doors operate through the Utility Hydraulic System," he yelled, barely audible above the engine noise, "If the Aux Air Doors don't open when you're on the ground, the engines will auto-accelerate to 100 percent."

We all gave him a blank look. He appeared disappointed.

"Okay, re-read your Dash One, page 7-1."

We all nodded.

When I got back to my room I looked at page

7-1. My eyes started to glaze over as I read about T2 Cutback, T2 Reset, T5 Reset and Auto Acceleration. And that was just on one page. I could see I was in a deep, deep pond, and would have to tread water, *really hard*, to not drown. This F-4 was one complex airplane, and I really would need to hit the books big time to have a handle on aircraft systems.

The Flight Manual, Tech Order 1-F-4E-1, was just short of 500 pages. We would need to master every page. And we weren't going to get our hands on an airplane until we had proven, through interminable written tests and simulator evaluations, that we were ready.

The Dash One contained hundreds of WARNINGs, CAUTIONs, and NOTEs. A WARNING was, "Operating procedures, techniques, etc., which will result in personal injury or loss of life if not carefully followed". A CAUTION was, "Operating procedures, techniques, etc., which will result in damage to equipment if not carefully followed". A NOTE was, “An operating procedure, technique, etc., which is considered essential to emphasize”. There were hundreds of them, and we had to prove we knew them all before we could get anywhere near the airplane.

Finally, after two weeks of ground school, we progressed to the simulator phase of training. In the simulator, we would learn our way around the cockpit and practice normal and emergency procedures.

The cockpit itself had the usual suite of flight instruments, which was dwarfed by the number of switches, controls and indicators for the systems we would use for tactical employment. Most of the switches had unique shapes, so that the pilot would know what switch he was operating without looking at it. The really important switches were on the stick grip and throttles, so the pilot could do everything he needed to do in combat without taking his hands off the throttles or stick. It was called HOTAS – Hands On Throttles And Stick.

During our simulator training we were given a Blindfold Cockpit Check. We had to close our eyes and identify every switch, control and indicator, by touch, without looking. There would come a time, our instructor told us, when we would need to keep our eyes on a target and select, arm and employ one of the many types of weapons the F-4 carries. Our lives may depend on us doing it correctly.

The ground school and simulator instructors were not the same as our instructors for flight training. Speedbrake, my buddy from DaNang, was my assigned IP for flight training. Finally, after what seemed like a lifetime, I would get my first flight in the F-4.

27

September 9, 1971

This was going to be my "Dollar Ride", my basic introduction to the airplane. Even though we were only going to fly for a little over an hour, and simply perform normal procedures, we briefed for two hours before we went out to the airplane.

Just strapping into the airplane was a cumbersome process that required assistance from the Crew Chief. There were Leg Restraining garters that had to be attached to upper and lower legs, to prevent the legs from flailing in the event of an ejection. There was the parachute harness that needed to be attached to the parachute, which was integrated into the ejection seat. No matter how flexible you were, you couldn't attach the parachute without assistance. Once fully strapped in, it was time to pull the pins on the ejection seat. Now the seat was "hot".

The ejection sequence could be initiated in one of several ways. There was an ejection handle at the front of the seat, right between the pilot's legs. Pull the handle, and you're ejecting. The other ejection handle was at the top of the ejection seat, right over the pilot's head. Pull down the handle and extend the face curtain to initiate the ejection. The third way for the pilot to eject was by having the WSO initiate the ejection by selecting the Open position on the Command Selector Valve and then ejecting. If the WSO ejected, after a very short delay the pilot would be automatically ejected, ready or not.

Emergency ground egress was a BOLD FACE emergency procedure we had memorized to the point that we could do it in our sleep. It was important to perform all of the steps in the correct order to ensure we wouldn't get hung up in the cockpit, or inadvertently actuate the ejection seat.

LOWER GUARD – UP

SHOULDER HARNESS – RELESASE

INSIDE HANDLE – ROTATE AFT

OUTSIDE HANDLE – LOCK UP

There were aspects of flying the F-4 that were different from the other airplanes I had flown. Before every takeoff, we would advance the throttles, one at a time, to check the engine instruments and exhaust nozzles. We checked them one at a time because the General Electric J79 engines produced so much thrust, 4000 pounds each, that the airplane would start sliding if we pushed both up at the same time, even if we were holding the brakes.

And if the pilot didn't want the airplane to move, he had to hold the brakes manually, since there was no parking brake. Because the engines produced so much thrust, even at Idle, we had to constantly put pressure on the brakes every time we were stopped. After any kind of extended ground operations, we would be physically drained before we even took off.

The takeoff procedure was to taxi into position on the runway, run each engine up separately and pull the throttle back to Idle, extend the flaps to the Takeoff position, pull the stick all the way back, and release the brakes while advancing both throttles to MIL and then pushing them outboard to the Afterburner detent and advance them all the way forward. The stick stayed all the way back until the nose came up to the takeoff attitude, early in the takeoff roll.

The acceleration was really amazing. Much greater than anything I had experienced up to this point. More than the T-38. Things happened pretty quickly, and as soon as the nose came up, I released back pressure and over-controlled a bit. I could feel Speedbrake on the controls with me.

Lift off, gear up, flaps up, accelerate on schedule. I had practiced it so much in the simulator, and in my head, that everything seemed to happen almost automatically. Then we practiced climbing on schedule, 10 degrees of pitch to reach 350 knots, maintaining 350 knots until reaching .90 Mach, then climb at .90 Mach, just shy of supersonic.

We entered the practice area, out over Biscayne Bay, at about 25,000 feet, and practiced performing turns with varying amounts of G-loading. During ground school the instructor had emphasized how we would need to keep the stick centered during high-G turns, but I wasn't a real believer until I experienced adverse yaw up close and personal.

"Let's go into a 3-G turn, and then increase the bank by another 10 degrees," Speedbrake instructed.

I rolled into a 70-degree bank to the right, stabilized, then moved the stick to the right, to get us up to a 6-G, 80-degree turn. BAM! The nose of the airplane snapped over to the left and the airplane was absolutely, totally, out of control. The horizon was moving in a manner I had never seen before, and I heard Speedbrake chuckling on hot mike.

"I have the airplane," he said.

I released the controls and watched the stick go full forward. Speedbrake was performing the Out-Of-Control Recovery Procedure, a procedure I had seen demonstrated in the instructional movie *Unload For Control.*

After some additional gyrations, and some uncomfortable negative Gs, the airplane recovered. We were at 15,000 feet. We had lost 10,000 feet faster than I could have imagined. Even though I thought I had a good sense of up and down, from my time as a gymnast at the Academy, I had been totally disoriented. I hadn't been able to read my altimeter during the gyrations, and if we had descended below 10,000 feet and still out of control, we would have been required to eject. It was a good thing Speedbrake was with me.

"I'm really glad that happened, Hamfist. We

can talk about adverse yaw all day long, but when you experience it in person, you really learn about it."

We climbed up to 25,000 feet again, while Speedbrake explained how to increase bank when in high-G conditions.

"Whenever you're at high G-loading, you keep the stick centered, totally centered. You fly *only* with your feet. Now let's try it again."

We practiced again, and again, and again. The first few times, I got a little wing wiggle as soon as I inadvertently had any aileron in the turn. After a few attempts, I got the feel for keeping the stick centered.

"You're not such a ham fist after all, Hamfist!"

28

September 9, 1971

We spent more time practicing maneuvers, then it was time to return for landing. Speedbrake briefed me pretty much nonstop as we entered the pattern.

We flew down Initial at 300 knots and pitched out into a 2-G turn. Abeam the touchdown point, gear down, maintain 250 knots. Slats and flaps down. Downwind until reaching the "perch", then 180 knots in the base turn. Halfway through the turn pick up the Indexer lights and fly AOA the rest of the way down to a firm landing.

Other than flying down Initial, which I had done at UPT, this was all new to me. The Indexer lights were visual Angle Of Attack – AOA – indicators located on each side of the windshield, right above the instrument panel. Having originated as a Navy plane, the F-4 flew approach using AOA. In addition to the Indexer lights, there was an aural AOA tone indication in our headsets. Above 15 units AOA, a 400 Hertz tone would sound in our headsets, beeping a little faster than once a second. As the AOA increased, the tone would beep faster and faster, with a shorter interval between beeps until, at approach AOA, it was as solid tone. When the AOA got higher than approach AOA, a 1600 Hertz tone would sound.

The tone took getting used to, but after a while it became second nature. During inflight maneuvering, I could be looking behind my aircraft and still know exactly what my AOA was all the time. Really neat.

The tone stopped as soon as the airplane landed. If you had an unbelievably smooth landing, you would know you were on the ground by the tone stopping.

But you weren't supposed to have smooth landings. Landings were supposed to be firm.

"This airplane was designed to land on aircraft carriers," Speedbrake explained, "When you land firmly, you instantly dissipate 20 knots of airspeed or more. Remember, no grease jobs."

29

October 1, 1971

On the fifth flight Speedbrake cleared me solo, and I flew with Deacon. During the time I had been getting my first few Transition flights with Speedbrake, Deacon had been receiving simulator training, learning to operate the Inertial Navigation System, the radar, and the weapons systems that were operated from the back seat. Deacon had one flight with Speedbrake to get the feel of flying in the F-4 before we flew together on our solo flight.

We flew a total of four Transition flights and nine Instrument flights, then I received a Transition check ride. Although it was called a Transition check, it was actually a combination Transition and Instrument check.

Learning to take off, fly instrument approaches and land the airplane was just the smallest part of our training. Now that the

Transition check was out of the way, it was time to learn how to employ the airplane. There was a lot to learn.

The airplane was a multi-mission fighter-bomber, which meant that it could do pretty much everything, other than carrying passengers. It could fly unlimited distances with aerial refueling. It could drop conventional bombs. It could fire missiles. It could fire a 20 millimeter Vulcan cannon. It could drop nuclear weapons. And we had to become proficient in performing all of those missions.

I would have preferred that we concentrate our training only on the things I would be doing in Vietnam. It was unlikely I'd be performing a nuclear weapons loft over there. But the syllabus had us learning everything, because not everyone in my class was headed to Vietnam. Most, in fact, were headed to Europe.

There were F-4 bases all over Europe, and

most of them had a role in the Cold War, that nuclear standoff with the Soviet Union. We had airplanes on nuclear alert all of the time, and jocks were constantly waiting for the Russian hordes to stream over the Fulda Gap, the trip wire that would start World War Three. I was glad I was headed back to Vietnam.

30

November 15, 1971

Once basic Transition and Instrument work were out of the way, it was time to re-learn how to fly formation. In this regard, the guys right out of UPT had a leg up on the rest of us. The T-38 was a much lighter airplane than the F-4, and was much touchier in pitch. As a consequence, the UPT guys had developed fine-tuned formation flying skills.

The rest of us hadn't flown formation for several years, and we were all pretty rough initially. It took three Formation rides for me to be cleared solo, which was right in line with the course syllabus.

Formation flying was the bread-and-butter of fighter flying. We flew in formation for everything we did. Depending on our munitions load and gross weight, we would either take off in formation or take off individually and then rejoin, but for the remainder of each mission we flew in formation.

We had to learn to employ the aircraft through the entire operating envelope. That meant high speed as well as low speed. Part of that training was to take the airplane to Mach 2.0, twice the speed of sound. Intuitively, I thought that all I would need to do to go Mach 2 was point the airplane down and advance the throttles. If I started from high enough, I should be able to reach Mach 2.

Wrong. If you go too fast at low altitude, where the air is dense, you will exceed the maximum dynamic pressure limit of the windscreen, the windshield. This was called the Q Limit. To minimize dynamic pressure, the aircraft had to be accelerated where the air was less dense, at higher altitude. So to get to Mach 2, we had to descend to pick up speed, then trade some of that speed for altitude while climbing to where the air was thinner and colder, and the speed of sound would be lower. So going Mach 2 would be at a slower speed, and at less dynamic pressure, than at sea level.

We also had to learn about a phenomenon called Mach Tuck. This occurred in the transonic region, just as the aircraft was accelerating to near-Mach speeds. Changes in the center of pressure of the swept wing, plus movement of the shock wave on the wing, would create a pitch-down tendency. Similarly, decelerating rapidly through the Mach would create a pitch-up tendency. There had actually been aircraft loss of control accidents when this pitch-up overstressed the aircraft that was rapidly decelerating through the speed of sound while in a turn, which had already created G-loading on the wing.

After Transition phase, we practiced Air Combat Maneuvering. ACM was dogfighting, and we practiced numerous scenarios. One versus one, called 1-v-1. We practiced 2-v-2, and 4-v-4. Sometimes we would start by approaching the enemy from behind, and let him practice trying to get us off his tail. Then we'd swap roles.

The more fun set-up was when we approached head-on. Then the fight would become a wild fur-ball. After I saw a 2-v-2 engagement from a distance, there was no question in my mind how aerial engagements had picked up the name “dogfight”.

In addition to ACM, we learned to perform aerial refueling. Once I had developed the touch for formation flying, I found refueling pretty easy. The challenging part was learning the Breakaway Maneuver, the emergency procedure that would need to be executed without hesitation if there was any problem during the refueling.

Unlike overseas, there were no MARS stations at stateside bases. That made it tough to get phone calls through to Sam. After I learned my way around base, I went to the

Wing Command Post and made friends with one of the shift commanders, Major Spencer "Sam" Spade. Sam would let me use the autovon at night to make calls to Yokota. That worked out perfectly, since it was daytime in Japan when it was night at Homestead.

In mid-November, Sam gave me a nice surprise.

"Ham, guess where I'm going on TDY."

"I hope it begins with H."

"You hoped right. I will be arriving at Homestead in time for us to have Thanksgiving together. I'll be there for a little over a month. We'll have our anniversary together also."

"That's fantastic!"

"Ham, I just can't wait to be with you again."

"Me too."

31

November 22, 1971

It was wonderful to have Sam with me while I was in training. At times, I had missed her so much I'd had trouble concentrating on my studies. And there was a lot of studying to do. Even though the flights only lasted a little over an hour, we briefed for two hours before every mission, and I usually studied for two or three hours before every briefing. And then I'd mentally re-fly each mission after every hour-long debriefing.

Then there were times when I didn't perform so well on my flights, and it was really great to have my soul-mate with me to spill my guts to after I screwed up. Sam hadn't seen me under pressure like this before. When I had been flying one or two-day trips out of Yokota, there was no stress at all. And when I was flying my missions in Vietnam, she wasn't around me. So this was a new experience, for both of us.

After ACM training, we learned how to drop bombs on the gunnery range. They weren't really bombs, they were training munitions called BDU-33s that somewhat simulated being bombs. The BDU-33 was a small blue bomb with a spotting charge that emitted a puff of smoke when the bomb hit the ground.

The BDU-33s were mounted on bomb racks on the wings, called either TERs or MERs. The TER was a Triple Ejector Rack, that held three bombs. The MER was a Multiple Ejector Rack, holding up to six bombs. The bombs were released from TERs and MERs by small explosive cartridges.

Once real bombs were released, they would arm only after a small propeller in the nose of the bomb had spun a sufficient number of times to arm the fuse. These propellers were prevented from spinning, and thus arming the bombs, while the bombs were on the aircraft, by wires that held them in place. When the bombs were dropped, the wires pulled out of the clips that ran through the small propellers and the bombs could arm.

We learned early that on every bombing mission it was essential for each airplane in the formation to look over the other aircraft, to make sure none of the bombs had "spinners". If there were spinners, the bombs would be armed while they were still on the airplanes, and any impact, such as a bird strike, would set off the bomb.

Our bombing training was performed at the Avon Park gunnery range, in central Florida. A Range Control Officer sat in a high tower and oversaw operations. From the tower, the RCO and his assistants would observe the white puff of smoke from each bomb delivery and, by observing from several vantage points and triangulating the impact position, would give us our score.

Typically, the score would be a distance and direction from the target, which was a prominent metal pyramid about 10 feet tall. Every now and then, someone would score a "shack", a direct hit. More often than not, our bombs would miss the target, but the distances for our misses gradually got smaller.

We all religiously kept track of our bomb scores, and computed our CEPs and CEAs after every gunnery mission. The CEP is the Circular Error Probable, the circular distance from the target that 50 percent of the bombs fall within. The CEA is the Circular Error Average, an arithmetic average of the circular distance from the target of all bombs dropped.

After learning to drop practice bombs on the manned gunnery range, we graduated to the Tactical Range, also located at Avon Park. The Tac Range was a man-made battlefield, with bunkers, tanks, trucks and other targets scattered all over the huge complex. Forward Air Controllers, usually student FACs, would control us on these targets and simulate actual combat conditions.

Late into our ground attack training, we practiced Full Scale Weapons Deliveries. For each FSWD mission, we carried 500-pound Mark-82 bombs with inert warheads. These were the same size and shape as real Mk-82s, with the same ballistics, but were filled with concrete instead of high explosives. The FSWD was our first introduction to heavy weight takeoffs, and takeoff speeds were higher, much higher, than we had experienced previously.

Well into our training we started night flying, practicing night formation and night weapons deliveries. Since most of my flying as a FAC had been at night, I assumed that this would be a piece of cake. There's a good reason for the expression, "Never assume".

I was totally out of my element. Other than knowing about dark vision adaptation and cockpit lighting, I was really a fish out of water.

There are precious few references for maintaining proper formation position at night, and turning rejoins were especially challenging. The F-4 was equipped with electro-luminescent lighting, which consisted of glowing strips on the wingtips and fuselage. That helped somewhat.

For our night weapons deliveries, we again worked with FAC students, who dropped ground markers and parachute flares. Frequently, the parachute flares, which would provide illumination for a few minutes, would extinguish just as we started our roll-in for the delivery. In an instant, the scene would go from bright illumination to pitch black. This was the real deal. It was something we'd be doing for a living in a few more months. It was tough, but it was great training.

In addition to air-to-ground and ACM, we did other air-to-air training. Since a lot of the guys were going to Europe, they had to be prepared to intercept the Russian bombers that would be ingressing Western Europe when the tanks crossed the Fulda Gap. So we learned how to perform intercepts and complete a maneuver called the Stern Conversion, in the clouds, relying solely on the radar.

Other than ACM, the most fun was firing on the dart. The dart was a wooden airfoil, 12 feet long and 4 feet wide, that was dragged 2000 feet behind the tow aircraft, another F-4, by a steel cable. Over the ocean gunnery range, we would approach the dart from a few miles behind, then make strafing passes with our 20 mm cannon. We took turns firing at the dart, while the tow aircraft stayed in a turn, so he wouldn't get hit by stray rounds. The dart was painted silver, and when it was hit it would sparkle as pieces of wood broke off.

Selecting the gun engaged the Lead Computing Optical Sight System. The LCOSS changed the gun sight pipper from a stationary dot to a constantly-moving aim point, changing with every movement and G-loading of the aircraft. As I went into a turn, the pipper would depress, to allow the gun to lead the target. It took a bit of time to get used to it

The plan was to make a dry pass, a pass without firing, for our first run, just to get a feel for the pacing. I was the first airplane to make a pass. Speedbrake, my IP in the back seat, got a radar lock on the dart, and was reading range information to me. We went through the weapons delivery checklist, which included selecting the Vulcan and moving the Master Arm switch to ARM, which allowed the Trigger Transfer Relay to prioritize guns over missiles.

Speedbrake called out range to target as we closed, and I set up for a firing solution, chasing the pipper and finally getting it right on the dart as we got in range. Speedbrake had been counting down distance to in-range, and then said, "Fire!" and I squeezed the trigger for a short burst. The dart sparkled.

"Shit!" Speedbrake shouted over the

interphone, "You were supposed to make this a dry pass. Well, at least you scored a hit."

I felt like an idiot for getting so fixated on the target that I had forgotten the instructions to make the first pass dry. But at the same time, I felt pretty good about scoring a hit.

After every live pass, we would perform a loose rejoin on the dart to see how many holes it had. At the end of the training period, the tow aircraft released the dart and it parachuted into the ocean.

It turned out I was the only student in our formation to score a hit, and I only got that one hit, on my first pass. Firing at a moving target was a lot tougher than it looked like in the movies.

32

December 25, 1971

We had a quiet anniversary celebration. It was nice to have a few days off, since I had been studying and flying pretty much nonstop the whole time Sam was at Homestead. At the same time, Sam had been staying pretty busy working out of the JAG Office on base.

We went to a nice restaurant, then got a room at the Hilton. Because the Billeting Office assigned two officers to each VOQ room, it had been hard for us to get private time for any degree of intimacy, other than renting an occasional hotel room.

Graduation was approaching, and my performance had been marginal, at best. I had felt immense pressure because of what Colonel West had told us about how some of the guys would wash out. So far, nobody had.

My bombs had been absolutely average. Not

the best, not the worst. My ACM was about the same. I had hit the dart, but it was on a pass I wasn't really supposed to fire from. All-in-all, I was a really mediocre fighter pilot.

The Ops Officer, Major Dunkle, called each of us into his office for a private chat toward the end of the course.

“Well, Hamfist, I have to be honest with you. I'm a bit disappointed in your performance, from what Speedbrake had told us about you.”

I really felt inadequate when I was around Major Dunkle. He was the epitome of the fighter pilot, and he consistently won all the money we wagered every time we went to the gunnery range. And, during the few times I'd done ACM against him, he'd smoked me every time.

“To be honest, sir, I'm disappointed also. Like everybody else, I had hoped to make Top Gun.”

Major Dunkle looked through my training

folder. Top Gun was the award for the best gunnery scores.

"Not a chance. You're right in the middle of the pack. You're not going to wash out or anything, but I gotta tell you, I don't think you'll ever be one of the guys who gets a MiG."

I bristled a bit at that. Like everyone else in the class who was headed to Vietnam, I was hoping to get, no, I was *going* to get a MiG.

"Well, Major, I think you're wrong about that, but time will tell."

"Okay, Hamfist, best of luck."

He shook my hand.

"Thank you, sir."

I saluted and started to leave his office. Then I turned to him from the office door.

"By the way, sir, after I return from Vietnam with my MiG-kill, I plan to come back here and wax your ass in ACM."

Major Dunkle broke out into a broad grin.

“I'll be waiting.”

33

February 20, 1972

Sam had gone back to Yokota after the first of the year, and we had been flying an eclectic mix of missions the final two months until graduation.

Because our class was so small, graduation was a really casual event. We all assembled in the squadron briefing room, and Colonel West came in and addressed us.

"Gentlemen, I want to congratulate you. You're the first class with a 100 percent graduation rate. That's a testament to your hard work and to your instructors."

He gave a glance of acknowledgement to the back of the room, where the instructors were assembled.

"You're now fully-qualified fighter pilots. That means you have a license to learn. With luck, you'll be flight leads in a year or two. I wish you all good luck and safe flying."

Then Colonel West stepped down from the podium and shook each of our hands. Next thing I knew, he was leaving the room.

"Room, atten-hut!"

We all snapped to attention, then, after Colonel West left, we shook hands with each other, and with each IP. Speedbrake came over to me and gave me a big hug.

"Damn, it was great working with you, Hamfist."

"Speedbrake, I want to thank you for everything. I feel like I let you down by not doing better."

"Good, better, best are all relative. You guys, all of you, are head and shoulders above where I was when I first became a fighter pilot. You're going to do great over there. And I have confidence in you – you're going to join me in the MiG-killer club."

I was now a fighter pilot. I was no longer strapping into the airplane, I was strapping it on, becoming one with the plane. But I had no misconceptions about being the World's Greatest Fighter Pilot, like it said on the commemorative coffee mug that Speedbrake had given me.

I had lot to learn, and I knew it.

34

February 21, 1972

Ever since my flight with the Army Green Beret, Major Warner, I had decided that if I ever went back to Vietnam on a combat tour I'd carry a Browning 9 millimeter semi-automatic, called the Hi-Power, with me, instead of the issued .38 caliber revolver. I knew from reputation that the Tamiami Gun Shop was the place to get a good price.

Early into my training at Homestead, I had stopped by the gun store and priced the Browning. It was $190 for the best model, the one with adjustable sights.

"How much would it be if I ordered several?" I asked.

"If you order 10, I can let you have them for $140 each."

It was time to see how good a salesman I

was. I went around to all the guys in my class, and a couple of guys in the follow-on class, who were headed to Vietnam, and told them about the deal. I told them about my experience with the 6-shot Air Force issue revolver, and I explained how the Browning carried 13 rounds, and could be reloaded much quicker than a revolver, even when injured.

It was an easy sell. Every guy I approached was interested, but they all had one big reservation.

"How do I get the gun to Vietnam?" asked one of the Lieutenants.

I was prepared for that question. I had gone to the Traffic Management Office and checked the shipment regulations. The Military Airlift Command regulations stated that we could ship our weapons in our hold baggage, the baggage that was sent ahead of us to Vietnam, as long as we had official orders authorizing shipment of a personal weapon.

I went to CBPO, the Base Personnel Office, and asked how I could get "shipment of personal weapon authorized" included in our PCD orders.

"Well, sir," said the Master Sergeant, "if the MAC regulation authorizes it, we'll put it in your orders."

Okay, it looked like we had a sort of standoff. CBPO wouldn't put the authorization in our orders unless the MAC regulation permitted it, and the MAC folks wouldn't permit it unless CBPO had the authorization in our orders. It was time for me to tie the two ends together.

I made a copy of the appropriate section of the MAC regulation and went to see the Officer In Charge of CBPO, Lieutenant Colonel Trapp.

"Sir, I need some help getting CBPO and TMO to talk together. TMO says they won't authorize shipment of my personal weapon unless it's in my orders. Your people tell me they can't put it in my orders unless TMO authorizes it. Can you help me?"

"Is this a joke?" he asked, as I handed him the copy of the TMO regulation.

I shook my head.

He read the TMO regulation over a couple of times, then dug out his regulation book and studied it for a few minutes.

"I can make this happen, Captain. Leave it to me. When are you leaving for Vietnam?"

"I graduate from RTU in February, sir."

He made some notes on a yellow legal pad on his desk.

"I'll take care of it. Give me a call as soon as CBPO tells you they're working on your orders."

CBPO would be contacting me before cutting my orders, to see if I would be requesting leave prior to going to Vietnam. I would.

"Thank you, sir. There will be other pilots

who would like it in their orders, also."

"Okay, Captain, Let me know their names, and I'll take care of it."

"Thank you, sir."

I left CBPO with a renewed respect for ground-pounders.

I had a short meeting with the guys who were interested in buying Brownings, and ended up with eleven guys who wanted to buy the guns. I called the Tamiami Gun Shop, placed the order, and we all went by and picked up our weapons a few days later. Then I took the list of gun owners to Lieutenant Colonel Trapp and he got "Shipment of personal weapon in hold baggage authorized" included in our orders.

I had requested a month of military leave after graduation, and that was put in my orders also. The orders assigned me a Port-Call from Travis Air Force Base, in Vacaville, California, on March 20th .

When I received my orders, I saw that I had been assigned to Ubon Royal Thai Air Base. I was thrilled. I had operated into Ubon numerous times with Scatback. Being based in Thailand was like being in a completely different world from Vietnam. Friendly people, no sappers, no rocket attacks.

But the best part was, Ubon was the home of the Eighth Tactical Fighter Wing. The 8th had earned its reputation as MiG-killers during Operation Bolo, when F-4s from the 555th Tactical Fighter Squadron, called the Triple Nickel, made their way into history books by downing seven MiGs in just a few days. If I played my cards right, I just may get into the Triple Nickel and get a chance at my own MiG.

There was one piece of business left. I needed to unload my car. I listed the Corvair in the base newspaper for sale for $300, and it sold the first day. So I had used the car for free for the past six months.

When I boarded the MAC flight to Travis, where I'd start my leave, I felt pretty proud of myself for taking care of the weapon transportation issue.

That feeling of pride lasted exactly one month.

35

February 21, 1972

You'd think that a guy with a tour in Vietnam, and another tour flying all over Asia, including Vietnam, would be pretty street-wise. You'd be wrong. I had so much to learn, I didn't even know how much I didn't know.

When I got to Travis, the first thing I did was go to the Scheduling Office at the Passenger Terminal and advise them to cancel my Port-Call, since I would be arranging for a Port-Call on my own from Yokota, where I'd be taking my month of leave. I showed my orders to the Sergeant, and he filled out some forms and gave me copies.

Next, I needed to send my hold baggage on ahead to Ubon. My hold baggage was all my civvies, uniforms, G-suit, helmet, flying gear, everything I would need at Ubon, but didn't want to lug around with me. And, of course, my

Browning. I put a copy of my orders in the A-4 bag that had my hold baggage, took the bag to the check-in desk, and put it on the scale.

"This is my hold baggage for Ubon, Airman," I said, as I handed him a copy of my orders. "I have a personal weapon in the bag, but it's authorized."

I pointed to the part of the orders that mentioned shipment of the weapon.

"All right, sir. I'll take care of it."

"Thank you."

For some reason, I had thought that bags were subject to x-ray screening, and I wanted to make sure that no one would think I was trying to smuggle my weapon overseas. What I had stupidly done, instead, was ensure that the weapon would never make it overseas.

The Airman took care of it.

36

March 21, 1972

My leave, of course, had seemed too short. I'd caught a Space-Available MAC flight to Yokota, and Sam and I had a wonderful month together. We went out to dinner with Tom and Miyako four times, and Sam had earned some Compensatory Time Off for some extra work she'd put in on some high-visibility projects, so we took a driving trip.

We headed south, and drove the entire length of Japan, ending up in Kyushu, the southern island.

"I want you to see Fukuoka, where I was born," she said.

So we went to Fukuoka and visited Itazuke Air Base. Itazuke had been made famous by the fighter pilot song, "Itazuke Tower", and it was really neat to see the base in person. During the Korean War, F-86 jocks had been stationed there, and had gone off to war, TDY, just like I had gone off to Vietnam, TDY. The more things change, the more they stay the same.

When I left Yokota for Ubon, it was different from the times I had gone to Vietnam. During the time I was with Scatback, we'd developed a routine for my departures. No more Gone-With-The-Wind farewell scenes, just resolute acceptance of our impending separation. We knew what it would be like.

Sam and I held each other for one last goodbye. A final kiss and I was on my way. As I boarded the flight, I looked back as Sam, Tom and Miyako waved to me, and again went off to war.

37

March 21, 1972

When I arrived at Ubon, The first thing I saw when I stepped off the plane was the sign that read, “Welcome To Ubon, Home of the Wolfpack”. I stood up a little straighter as a feeling of pride and anticipation surged through me. This was what I'd been hoping for, planning for, training for.

I checked in at the Information counter at the terminal, and the Sergeant provided me with my squadron assignment. It wasn't the 555th. I guess the disappointment showed on my face.

“Were you expecting to be assigned to the Triple Nickel, sir?”

“Actually, I was.”

“We see a lot of that, sir. The Triple Nickel isn't at Ubon anymore. They relocated to

Udorn a couple of years ago."

I was processing this unexpected information, when I heard someone call my name.

"Hamfist!"

I turned around, and there, in the flesh, was Vince, my former room-mate from the Academy, the SAR pilot who had picked me up so many times!

We hugged each other like long-lost sorority sisters.

"Vince! How long have you been here? What squadron are you in?"

"I've been here two months, and I'm in the same squadron as you, the 25th. In fact, as soon as I saw you were assigned to us, I told the Squadron Admin guy we *had* to be room-mates. And he made it happen."

"That's fantastic."

"I have a lot to tell you about our operation. Let's get you settled, and then we'll go to the club and talk. Your hold baggage has been in the squadron storage room for a few weeks."

We went to the squadron and I made the usual round of introductions. These guys would be my brothers for the next 12 months. Vince took me to the storage room, grabbed my A-4 bag and handed it to me.

"Here's your hold baggage, Hamfist."

Something felt not quite right about my A-4 bag. I had put a padlock on the zipper closure, and now it was gone. I had a really sick feeling about this. I opened the bag, and all my flying gear was still there. But the gun was gone.

There were a few loose cartridges scattered in the bottom of the bag, but the weapon and the box of cartridges were missing. I told Vince about the gun.

"Vince, do you think anyone got to my bag while it was in storage?"

"No way, Hamfist. I received the bag the minute TMO said it had arrived, and it was exactly like this. There was no lock on the bag when they delivered it, and our squadron is really secure."

For the Browning, the operation was a success, but the patient died. I had done everything right up to the last minute, then I blew it by being such a naïve boy scout. I had been programmed, from four years at the Academy, with its Cadet Honor Code, to think that everyone was honest. Even with a tour in Vietnam, I hadn't learned much about the real world.

Okay, no use crying over spilt milk. I got my bags unpacked, and Vince took me to the O'Club. I would need to report the stolen weapon to the JAG Office, but that could wait.

"You're going to love our flying here. We have great missions, and we carry a great mix of bombs. Mark-82, CBUs, LGBs."

"What's an LGB?"

"Laser Guided Bomb. They're incredible. You drop it like a regular bomb, and it guides to the target when the FAC illuminates it with a laser. It's something right out of Star Trek."

"Very cool."

We talked on for a couple of hours. Vince had gotten an F-4 assignment to Europe after his tour at NKP, and then volunteered for a second tour.

"Are many of the guys in the squadron on their second tours?" I asked.

"A bunch. In fact, there are some guys on their third tour. We have a great group of guys."

Vince looked at his watch.

"I'm supposed to take you to meet Colonel Holder in about a half hour."

"Okay. Who's he?"

"Lieutenant Colonel Robert Holder. He's our Ops Officer. Hates his nickname."

"Don't tell me it's Dick."

"Give that man a cigar! He's a really good guy, dyed in the wool fighter pilot. Flew Huns his last tour."

The "Hun" was the F-100, a real fighter-pilot's airplane, single seat. The Hun was being phased out of the active inventory, replaced by F-4s. Even though the F-4 could do more, it was a shame to see Huns go.

We went back to the squadron, and Vince escorted me into Lieutenant Colonel Holder's office.

"Welcome to the 25th, Hamfist."

"Thank you, sir. It's a real pleasure to be here."

"You wouldn't be bull-shitting me, would you? Everybody who comes to Ubon thinks they're going to get into the Triple Nickel."

“Well, sir, actually the thought had crossed my mind...”

“I understand completely. But I'm going to let you in on a little secret. When we start bombing the north again, and we *will* start bombing the north again, we're going to be the bombers. And you know who gets to see the MiGs? The bombers.”

“The MiG-Cap,” he continued, “might fly along for hours, looking for trouble, maybe go for days without making contact. Every mission, we drop our bombs, roll up and take a look at our results. Instant feedback, instant gratification.”

“And there's the chance,” he smiled, “we'll probably see more MiGs than the MiG-Cap guys.”

“I'm looking forward to getting started flying, sir.”

“Well, it'll take a little while. Things are very structured around here now. You have to go to

Wing Indoc for some briefings before you can start flying, but we'll get you on the schedule as soon as we can."

"Thank you, sir."

I left his office feeling really optimistic.

Later in the day, I went to the JAG Office and filed a report about the missing weapon. They put me in contact with a Captain from the Office of Special Investigations.

The OSI was the Air Force equivalent of the FBI, and they treated the matter with a great deal of seriousness.

"Do you remember the name of the Airman you checked your bag with?"

It had been a month since I had checked the bag, and I'm not sure I had even paid attention to his name at the time. I felt like a total idiot.

"No."

"Well, we'll advise our office at Travis and

see what we can come up with, but it doesn't look too promising."

"Okay. Thanks for anything you can do."

I would eventually be reimbursed the cost of the Browning. The money wasn't my chief concern. Weapons were not permitted to be imported into Thailand, so now there was no way I could get my hands on a Browning again. I learned my lesson, and it was a tough one.

Local area training was fairly involved. There were several briefings I attended with other FNGs, and several written exams. The Wing, rightfully, wanted us to know the local area, including major diversion airfields, down cold. In my own case, I had flown to all of them with the Scatback operation, but the training was highly structured, and there wasn't any allowance made for prior experience. I was anxious to get flying, but I would have to wait.

I needn't have worried. The war wasn't going anywhere without me.

38

April 13, 1972

Finally, I was scheduled for my first combat mission. The birds at Ubon were F-4Ds, which meant that they didn't have the internal gun. Other than that, I couldn't tell much difference. A little later, some TDY F-4Es arrived, and we flew them all interchangeably.

Springs Springer, a Fighter Weapons School graduate, was my IP in the back seat for my checkout. Springs was really an old head. Although he was still a Captain, he was already on his third tour in F-4s.

Springs gave me a thorough briefing on the base facilities, which I had already known, the target area, which I knew somewhat, and the weapons, which I knew about but had never dropped.

We were carrying snake and nape. Mark-82 high-drags and napalm. There was a lot of fighting in the An Loc area, and we would be launched single ship to rendezvous with a FAC. We were actually going to fly three sorties on this mission.

We were fragged to fly to An Loc for our first employment, then recover at Bien Hoa to refuel and load more bombs, and work the An Loc area again. After that, we'd recover one more time at Bien Hoa, refuel, reload and work a target in Laos on our way back to Ubon.

Three flights in one day. Now we're talking! At Indoc, they said I'd need ten missions to be considered combat ready. Three days like this and I'd be almost there.

There were Troops In Contact at An Loc, and they really needed our help. I couldn't see much on the ground to see who were the good guys and who were the bad guys, but the FAC gave us a good mark, and I had all my bombs on target. No secondaries, but I didn't expect any with TIC. Results Not Observed.

Obviously, the FAC knew what he was doing. The rules said that a FAC didn't estimate Killed By Air numbers. Unless there was an actual body count, there was no KBA. Simply RNO.

We recovered at Bien Hoa, left our gear in the airplane, and went into the ready room to get a snack while they prepped our airplane for the next flight. In the ready room, there was a long table with sandwiches, desserts, soft drinks and coffee. It seemed the airplane was ready to go before I had even finished my first sandwich.

Back to An Loc. Same target area, still TIC. This time, I just had Mk-82s, sixteen of them. Again, all bombs on target. Again, RNO. RTB at Bien Hoa one last time.

This time we were loaded with Mk-82s and CBU-24s. We took off and headed northwest, to rendezvous with a FAC over Steel Tiger. Although Steel Tiger had been my old Area of Operations, we were in the Pleiku FAC AO, south of my old hunting grounds, and I didn't recognize any of the targets.

The Pleiku Covey put us in on a suspected truck park, and we got several secondary explosions. It was like Lieutenant Colonel Holder had said. I dropped my bombs – they were great – and rolled up to see my handiwork. Instant gratification.

When I landed at Ubon, I was physically drained, but mentally pumped. We went to the squadron for a short debriefing, and then we were done for the day.

When I left the briefing room, the Captain from the OSI was waiting to see me. I figured he might have information about my stolen Browning.

I was wrong.

39

April 13, 1972

The Captain from the OSI was there to interview me regarding my being charged with the military crime of Missing Movement.

Apparently, the Sergeant at the Scheduling Office at Travis had dropped the ball, and left my name on the flight manifest for my original Port Call from Travis to Ubon. When I didn't show up for the flight, the Passenger Service Department issued an All Points Bulletin for me. They thought I was a deserter, while I was flying combat missions!

I showed the OSI Captain the copies of my Port Call cancellation, and he said he'd take care of everything. One thing I'd learned at the Academy, and I learned it well, was to hold onto every piece of paper with my name on it.

"Even if it's just a short note," The Sergeant at Graduation Out-processing had advised me, "if your name is on it, hold onto it forever. Someday you'll thank me."

I said a silent, "Thank you, Sarge."

I flew several more triple-turns to Bien Hoa over the next several days, and then took a combat check ride.

The check ride was simply a normal combat mission, with a WSO in the back seat, and the check pilot flying on my wing. It was great to be leading the flight, something I'd done only a few times in training, and may not get to do for quite a while, since only the most experienced pilots would upgrade to Flight Lead.

My bombs were great, and the check pilot said I did a good job. Based on my bombs, I had expected him to say I did an outstanding job, but no such luck.

"Your bombs were excellent, Hamfist," he said, "but you need to put more effort into thinking about your wingman when you lead. You had me down-sun during most of the flight to the target, when you should have put me up-sun. And when you made turns, your roll-ins were not very smooth."

I could see I had a lot to learn.

40

May 2, 1972

This was my first mission over North Vietnam. If my WSO hadn't told me, I never would have known we weren't still over South Vietnam. No big red line on the ground to mark the DMZ, the border between North and South Vietnam. No difference in the terrain. Not even much difference in the enemy reaction, mostly just triple-A.

It hadn't always been that way with enemy reaction. About six months earlier, southern North Vietnam, Route Pack One, was as bad as the Hanoi area, Route Pack Six. Airfields with MiGs, SAMs, wall-to-wall triple-A. And then the F-105 Wild Weasels, in coordination with the Wolfpack airplanes, had used the "roll-back" tactic of attacking the threats at the periphery of the defended area and incrementally destroying the threats in the area, gradually increasing the area considered lower threat.

By the time I flew over Route Pack One, it was hardly more dangerous than Laos. Meaning – you can get your ass shot down any day of the week, but no MiGs or SA-2s.

We worked with an OV-10 FAC, Musket 3. Our target was a storage area, and I was carrying 16 Mark-82s. I made six passes, a thousand pounds of bombs per pass, and I had good bombs. No, I had great bombs. We got three secondaries, and the FAC sounded ecstatic.

While we were orbiting the target, my WSO, an old head close to DEROS named Cliff Clifford, pointed out the two prominent landmarks that distinguish southern North Vietnam: Bat Lake and Fingers Lake.

Bat Lake was shaped just like a bat's wings, and Fingers Lake looked like the outstretched fingers of a hand. Nobody ever accused fighter pilots of being overly creative, but the names worked. Even when most of the ground was obscured by clouds, if you caught a glimpse of Bat Lake or Fingers Lake, you instantly knew where you were.

North Vietnam was divided into "Route Packages" that had numbers starting at the DMZ, similar to the way South Vietnam was divided into Military Region I (formerly called I Corps), MR II, MR III, etc.

Route Pack One started at the DMZ, and Route Pack Two was north of Route Pack One, and the numbering continued northward to Route Pack Six, the Hanoi area.

Route Pack Six was the most heavily defended area in the world. There was wall-to-wall triple-A of every caliber, SA-2 radar-guided SAMs with a range of over 20 miles, SA-7 heat-seeking SAMs, and, of course, MiGs.

The name MiG was an abbreviation for the names of the Russian designers, Mikoyan and Gurevich, small letter "i" being the Russian word for "and". Like every other weapon the North Vietnamese – and, for that matter, the Chinese – had, the MiG was a Soviet-designed aircraft. The MiGs came in several flavors.

The MiG-17 was an older aircraft, but still lethal. It had a highly swept wing and could turn really well at low speed. The MiG-17 had a 27 millimeter cannon with 80 rounds and a 37 millimeter cannon with 40 rounds. Either cannon was capable of blowing you out of the sky in a heartbeat. It was subsonic, had a range-only radar, and didn't carry missiles. Its weakness was its manual elevator control. Although the ailerons were hydraulically powered, the elevator wasn't, which meant that the faster it went, the harder the pilot had to pull on the stick to turn. If you had a MiG-17 on your tail and went fast and went into a hard turn, the airplane itself was capable of turning with you, but the pilot – especially a little hundred-pound North Vietnamese pilot – probably wouldn't be strong enough to pull on the pole with enough force to stay with you in the turn. If you got a MiG-17 on your tail at low altitude, the best tactic was to go into a steep dive and pick up tons of airspeed. Then, pull out just before impacting the ground. The F-4 can make the pullout. The MiG-17 can't. A kill's a kill.

The MiG-19 was its newer brother. It was twin-engine, like the F-4, it was supersonic, like the F-4, and had hydraulic flight controls, like the F-4. In addition to its cannon, it also carried two Atoll air-to-air heat-seeking missiles, similar to our AIM-9s. It was fast and maneuverable. Really lethal. It could out-turn an F-4, and you would be really stupid to get into a turning dogfight with one.

The newest aircraft, the MiG-21, had a delta-wing planform. Like the MiG-17 and MiG-19, it was single seat. It was fast, it had a cannon and two Atoll missiles, and it too was extremely lethal. Its main weakness was forward visibility – it had a front windscreen with the transparency of a coke bottle.

I had a hard time with enemy aircraft recognition, and remembering the strengths and weaknesses of the different model MiGs. But it was important for me to learn them.

My life might well depend on it.

41

May 5, 1972

I was Number Two in Dingus Flight, working with a Nail FAC in Laos. Each of us had Mark-82s and CBU-24s. The FAC had found a truck park along the trail.

The airstrike was going great. First, the FAC put us in with our Mark-82s, to blow away the triple canopy cover, and I was about to make my first run-in with CBUs. I was in a 135-degree bank, pulling my nose through toward the target for a 45-degree delivery, when I heard the distress call on Guard, followed by a single beeper.

"Wolf 41 is hit! Bailing out over Bat Lake!"

I had been to breakfast with Vince about two hours before my flight briefing.

"What kind of mission are you on today, Vince?"

"It's my checkout as a Fast FAC. After I saw all the fun you were having as a FAC, I decided I wanted to see what it's all about. I'll be flying with Sambo."

Sambo Sampson was one of the most experienced pilots in the squadron. He was on his third tour. He had been a Covey and a Raven, and now was a Fast FAC in the F-4. I knew Vince would have a great role model for his Fast FAC work.

Sambo's call sign was Wolf 41.

When I heard Wolf 41 go down, I had the sick feeling in the pit of my stomach that I'd had so many times in the past. If I had heard two beepers, I would have felt a little better. But I only heard one. That meant there was only one good chute, since the opening of the parachute triggered the beeper.

I completed my roll-in, let the pipper track up to the target, and pickled off my CBU. I had to compartmentalize. There was nothing I could do right now for Vince, and if I dwelled on his situation, I might make a mistake that could cost one of the guys in my formation, or the FAC, his life. My CBU delivery was perfect, and I had a momentarily thought what an insensitive asshole I must be, to drop my bombs like there was nothing wrong. But it was what I had to do. I had to compartmentalize.

Back when I was in pilot training, at Laughlin, in 1968, I wasn't so good at compartmentalizing. Neither were most of my classmates. Our Class Leader was Charlie Higgins. Charlie was the Class Leader by virtue of his rank. He was a Captain among all of us Second Lieutenants.

Charlie had been a Bombardier-Navigator on B-52s. During an Operational Readiness Inspection, he had done everything right, but at the last minute there had been an equipment malfunction, and his bomb missed the target on the training range. Missed it by a mile. Charlie's crew was being chewed out by the

Brigadier General who had been overseeing the ORI.

Actually, it was the Aircraft Commander of Charlie's crew that was being chewed out. Being a pilot, the Aircraft Commander was responsible for everything that happened on his mission.

During a break in the ass-chewing, Charlie spoke up.

“General, the bad bomb was entirely my fault. There was nothing the Aircraft Commander could have done. I accept full responsibility.”

There was a moment of stunned silence, then the General spoke.

“Captain, if you want to accept responsibility, you're wearing the wrong kind of wings.”

A week later, Charlie had an assignment to pilot training.

Being a Captain, Charlie really knew his way around the Air Force, and was really a great role model. We all looked forward to his weekly bullshit sessions.

And, on this particular day in 1968, Charlie washed out of pilot training. Although Charlie know a lot about the Air Force, and Aviation Meteorology, and Aerodynamics, and lots of other things we had to learn, Charlie just couldn't fly.

The day Charlie washed out we all performed terribly. Including me, and I went on to become Distinguished Graduate. We were all thinking about poor Charlie, when we should have been thinking about our flying.

Our Section Commander, a grizzled old Major who had been an IP for over ten years, called a special meeting of all the students.

"You all did really shitty today. And that's just not acceptable. I know you all feel bad about Captain Higgins, but that's the breaks.

He may have been a great guy, and maybe even a great leader, but he was a shitty pilot. If you were on his wing in combat he could get you killed. So, if you want to feel bad for him, you do it on your own time."

"When you're flying a million-dollar Air Force aircraft, you can't afford the luxury of anything other than total concentration and commitment to your mission. There will come a time in your career when your best friend will get shot down off your wing, and you'll need to be able to put it out of your mind and get on with the mission. If you can't do that, you can join Captain Higgins and get the hell out of pilot training."

So we learned to compartmentalize. We learned to focus. We learned to put everything out of our minds except the mission.

There would be time for me to grieve for Vince. I would be his Summary Courts Officer. There would be time for me to cry, in the solitude of my room, or in the shower, or in the steam room at the base gym. Places no one would see me.

But, right now, all that mattered was getting my bombs on target, looking out for threats, and completing the mission.

42

May 10, 1972

The previous night, the squadron Scheduling Officer had gone up to each of us, individually, at the Officer's Club, where we gathered pretty much every night.

"There will be a mass briefing at 0400 tomorrow, Wing Headquarters. It's a Special."

I'd heard about Specials. There had been some Specials a few months earlier, before I had arrived, for high-priority SARs. There had even been a Special for a single-ship mission into Pack Three, to implant sensors for the Igloo White Program.

This sounded like it was going to be something important, and I had a hard time getting to sleep. I set my alarm clock for 0230, shut my eyes, and at some point drifted off.

When the alarm woke me, for a minute I had

forgotten that I was alone in the room.

"Vince. Time to wake up".

Then I remembered. Vince was gone. Focus, Hamfist, focus.

I went to the O'Club for breakfast, ate quickly, and walked to Wing Headquarters. About half of the guys were already in place in the mass briefing room, and there was nervous chatter as we all waited to see what was in store. Finally it was 0400.

"Wing, atten-hut!"

The Wing Commander entered the room, escorted by a Major from the Intel Department.

"Take your seats, gentlemen," the Wing Commander said, "Today, we are initiating Operation Linebacker, an aerial bombardment campaign against North Vietnam. Our wing will be conducting the bombing, with 2000-pound Mark 84 Laser Guided Bombs. Each of our sixteen flight leads will have target illumination gear. Major Wright will now brief the targets."

A tall, thin Major stood at the front of the room, as a map of downtown Hanoi was projected on the large screen. There were sixteen red triangles on the map, designating the targets for each flight. A Lieutenant from Intel was passing out lineup cards, the small cardboard sheets that contained all of our strike information, such as target coordinates, strike frequency, Time Over Target, refueling information, and aircraft tail numbers. There were sixteen sets of lineup cards, one for each flight.

Actually, there was another set of lineup cards. The ground spare pilot was issued sixteen lineup cards. If any airplane aborted, the ground spare would fill in for him. I was scheduled to be the ground spare.

The Major started out his briefing with a time hack, and then covered every target in detail, including run-in direction and TOT. This strike of sixteen four-ships was going to be a highly orchestrated event. If any flight was early, or late, to the target, the whole thing could turn into a giant fur-ball.

After the mass briefing, we returned to our squadron for individual flight briefings. As the ground spare, I briefed with Maple Flight, led by our Squadron Commander, Lieutenant Colonel Wiley.

At the appointed time, I went out to my aircraft with my WSO, Pete Peterson, and we preflighted the airplane and bombs. This was the first time I'd carried Mk-84Ls. Huge, impressive bombs, with a swiveling laser seeker head.

I cranked up and taxied over to the holding pad on the far side of the runway. I would have my bombs armed right before takeoff if I was going to launch. So there I sat, holding the brakes, while all sixteen four-ships taxied out, armed up, and took off.

Holding the brakes for over an hour was tough, really tough. Even at Idle power, the F-4 wanted to move forward. It was like a prize fighter anxious to get into the ring.

When all of the strike aircraft had taken off, it was a lonely feeling. I taxied back to the parking revetment, shut down, and went back to the squadron.

The Squadron Duty Officer, Pete Peterson and I sat in the building and waited. We waited for our brothers to return.

43

May 10, 1972

We didn't have to wait very long. An entire sortie from Ubon to Hanoi and back only lasted a little over two hours. Takeoff, hit the tanker, ingress the target, drop bombs, egress the target, refuel, RTB. So much to do in so little time.

We could tell the guys were back before they had even entered the building. There was loud talking, faster than normal. Nervous energy filled the room, and it was like there was electricity in the air. After everybody had gone to Life Support to hang up their parachute harnesses and put their helmets on the cleaning rack, everyone headed to the O'Club.

Pete and I followed them to the bar, feeling like total outsiders. There were stories, lots of stories. Everyone telling about the SAMs, the triple-A, the MiGs they saw. Yes, they saw

MiGs.

Springs Springer was passing out River Rat applications to all the pilots who had flown on the mission. The River Rats, formally known as the Red River Valley Fighter Pilots Association, was a fraternal group open only to crewmembers who had flown over Pack Six. Having a River Rat patch on your flight suit was a major status symbol. Springs passed out a patch to everyone who completed his River Rat application.

Someone put a quarter in the juke box and selected record B-6. As soon as the music started playing, everyone stopped talking.

A long, long time ago, I can still remember how that music used to make me smile...

We all listened to *American Pie*, and, when the refrain sounded, everyone joined in.

This will be the day that I die, this will be the day that I die.

Fortunately for all of us, not today.

44

May 11, 1972

This was day two of Linebacker, and I would get to fly. My WSO was Johnnie Johnson, a lanky Lieutenant from Georgia who had been on the Linebacker mission the previous day, so he was considered an "old head". I had flown a few sorties with Johnnie, and I liked having him as my back-seater. Nothing rattled him.

The morning briefing started with a change to the Rules of Engagement.

"The ROEs are changed now," stated the Wing Commander. "Yesterday, we had an F-4 shoot at another F-4. Thank God he missed. But we can't have any more of that."

"Effective immediately," he continued, "any camouflaged airplane is off limits. I don't care if it's a MiG with Ho Chi Minh's picture on the tail, if it's camouflaged, it's off limits. Any questions?"

No one had any questions. Besides, this ROE was overkill. Everyone knew that MiGs were silver. Always silver. Not a problem.

The target for our flight, Dingus Flight, was the Bac Mai Airfield. We were each carrying two Mk-84Ls, 2000-pound laser guided bombs, and our lead was our Squadron Commander, Lieutenant Colonel Wiley. I was Dingus Two, in an F-4E.

It was fairly customary for the FNG to be Number Two in the formation. He would be right next to Lead, and Lead could keep an eye on him and try to help keep him out of trouble. Being Number Two was a comforting feeling, kind of like having an older brother put his arm around your shoulder.

We departed as the sun rose, the last flight to take off, joined up and headed north to refuel on Green anchor. I was tucked in securely on Lead's right wing. We took on our fuel, then silently flew alongside the tanker to the drop-off point, periodically cycling back into the pre-contact position to top off. Unlike the last time I had refueled, when I was at RTU, all of our refueling was done in total radio silence.

We dropped off the tanker, spread out to tactical formation with 1500 feet spacing, and ingressed the target area. There were fifteen strike flights ahead of us, and as soon as we switched over to strike frequency, there was total pandemonium on UHF.

For some reason, probably because of my apprehension, it reminded me of Hell Night at my high school fraternity. On Hell Night, all of us pledges were blindfolded and hooked together with a rope tied around each of our waists as we blindly stumbled along, pulled by the upperclassmen to our punishment.

The paddling had started. I could hear the whack of the paddles as they hit the pledges ahead of me, and I could hear the upperclassmen yelling and the pledges screaming out. I hadn't been hit yet, but the sound of the impending beating scared the shit out of me. In some respects, the anticipation was worse than the paddling itself.

Now, inbound to Hanoi, I was hearing sounds I'd never heard before, the frantic calls of the flights ahead of us. The sounds gave me chills.

"Maple Flight, SAM, SAM, Break right!"

"Walnut Two, move it around! Triple-A has you bracketed!"

"Elm Three is hit! Bailing out!"

Then the high-to-low sound of a beeper on Guard. A bit later, a transmission on Guard, barely comprehensible due to wind noise.

"Elm Three Alpha has a good chute. I think my arm is broken."

More SAM calls. More triple-A calls. MiG calls. A lot of transmissions garbled, as one radio call blanked out another.

Then, perhaps 5000 feet above us, a MiG-21 flew left to right just ahead of us. It was silver, and looked exactly like a Revell model airplane. I have no idea what he was doing. He wasn't in an engagement with anyone. He was just flying along, straight and level. Easy pickings for someone.

All I could think was, "Arm the missiles, raise the nose, and blow that son of a bitch out of the sky," but I maintained my position. My job was to stay in formation. Our job was to get the bombs on Bac Mai Airfield.

I had been totally unprepared for what to expect Hanoi to look like. I suppose I thought it would be a large city with a lot of vertical development. But it was flat, no tall buildings at all. We were already over Hanoi and I didn't even know it.

"Dingus Flight, arm 'em up."

I reached down and raised the Master Arm

switch on the lower instrument panel. Lead rocked his wings, to bring us into close fingertip formation for the delivery. I started easing over to the left to get into position.

Just then Johnnie, unflappable Johnnie, was screaming on the intercom.

“We got a SAM at four o'clock! Break right! BREAK RIGHT!”

When unshakeable Johnnie has a voice with a higher octave than the aural AOA tone, I know he's serious. I broke right, looking for the SAM.

“I don't see it, Johnnie.”

“It's coming right at us! BREAK RIGHT! HARDER!”

I pulled harder on the pole, turning hard right with the aural AOA sounding a steady tone.

“Okay, it's past us,” he said. “Let's get back into formation.”

I turned back to the left, and my formation was gone. While I had been breaking right, they were rolling in to the left. Off to my left, I saw the remains of a large orange airburst.

I looked down, saw the distinctive triangular runway pattern of the Bac Mai Airfield, and rolled in, resetting my gun sight to the ballistic mill setting for my Mk-84s, instead of the centroid settings preferred when the bombs would be guided by a laser. They were now just going to be gigantic dumb bombs.

I pulled off target and breathed a sigh of relief. I'd gotten my bombs on target. Now it was time to get the hell out of town.

“Johnnie, give me steering to the egress point.”

He already had it programmed in the INS.

“It's on the number one needle, Hamfist.”

“Okay,” I said, “Let's get the fuck out of here.”

I really had to take a piss.

45

May 11, 1972

We headed west to the egress point, south of Thud Ridge. Our route was going to take us back over Laos, then south to the tanker and on to Ubon. The airstrike was over. All of the strike aircraft had exited the target area.

Except me. I was all alone over downtown Hanoi. And, just like in every World War Two movie where the German fighters would attack the stragglers, I was the lone target for every enemy gunner in the area. We had another SAM shot at us, this time from our left eight o'clock. It went wild, and didn't even come close. There was a lot of triple-A. Triple-A I could deal with. Big sky.

Then Johnnie was screaming again.

"Break right! It's a fucking Atoll!"

I broke hard right again, aural tone

sounding continuously. Our airspeed was bleeding off at 50 knots per second from the heavy G-loading.

"Okay," Johnnie announced, "It's past us. That fucking MiG just shot at us with a fucking Atoll missile!"

I was fast approaching the proverbial point where I was out of airspeed, altitude and ideas. I checked my fuel. My external wing tanks were empty, and I reached over to the left subpanel and jettisoned them. I unloaded to about a half-G, lit min burner and accelerated. We needed to get the fuck out of the target area.

Finally, we were at the egress point. I breathed a sigh of relief and switched over to post-strike frequency.

"Dingus Two is up."

Lead sounded surprised.

"Dingus, Two," he called, "say your pigeons to Udorn."

I tuned up the Udorn TACAN and gave him my radial and DME.

"Take up a heading of 175, Dingus Two. We're eight miles ahead of you."

I turned to 175 and looked out ahead of my aircraft. It was probably the first time I'd even paid attention to anything outside the aircraft since my first SAM break, other than on my bomb delivery. Off in the distance, ahead of me, I could see two aircraft. I assumed that one of the other Dingus aircraft was no longer in the formation.

"Dingus Lead, this is Two. I have your two aircraft in sight."

"No, Two, there are three in our flight. Everyone except you managed to stay in formation. Get your ass back up here."

He sounded pissed.

"Roger."

I looked again. No, it was just two aircraft.

Then I saw, well ahead of the two aircraft, a flight of three F-4s. There were two aircraft closing in on the six o'clock of Dingus Flight!

I pushed the power up to close on the two aircraft. I was able to discern the distinctive cruciform tails of two MiG-17s.

"Johnnie, those are two MiGs following our flight. Get a lock up and give me range information."

Johnnie got a lock on the two targets and was reading distance and angle off to me.

This was the moment Fate had designed for me and me alone. I was single-ship in an F-4E, with an internal gun. I had recently qualified, okay, semi-qualified, on the dart. I was at the six o'clock of two MiGs. I may have fucked up royally up until now, being broken off from my formation, but this was my time to bag one, no, two, MiGs.

I didn't have to piss any more. I wanted to get my rocks off. As I closed, I saw one of the

MiGs dip his left wing, then both started turning hard left.

I've never seen airplanes turn that quickly. One minute I was looking at their tails, a few seconds later I was looking at their planforms. I performed a high-speed yoyo and closed to firing range, chasing my LCOSS toward my target, the MiG wingman. As I got in range, I saw that they were, indeed, MiG-17s, with red stars on their tails. But, damn it, they were camouflaged!

I had about three milliseconds to make a decision. Instantly, I mentally heard a replay of Colonel West, telling us that flight discipline was the most important quality for a fighter pilot to have. And I heard our Wing Commander, telling us in no uncertain terms that camouflaged aircraft were off limits.

“Shit!” I exclaimed, “They're camo.”

I performed a quarter roll and zoom maneuver, headed south, and rejoined my formation. Dingus Flight had been oblivious to the entire engagement.

"Shit, shit, shit!"

After we landed, I reported the camouflaged MiG-17s to Intel, and everyone in Dingus Flight gave disapproving sighs. *This FNG doesn't know what the hell he's talking about.* Later that day, several of the MiG-Cap flights from Udorn reported seeing camouflaged MiG-17s, and the ROE was changed the next day. We would be able to, again, fire at camouflaged MiGs.

Following the Intel debrief, Lieutenant Colonel Wiley called me into his office and shut the door.

"What happened out there, Hamfist?"

"Just as our flight was rolling in on the target," I replied, "we had a SAM from our four o'clock. Johnnie called it. It was tracking us, and I had to break right or we would have been hit."

"Well," he said, "in all honesty, I thought you had been shot down. I looked over to where you were supposed to be when I rolled in, and all I saw was a SAM detonation. I was really surprised when you came up on post-strike frequency."

"I really don't want my wingmen breaking out of my formation," he said, as he walked me to the door of his office, "but if you *really* have to, at least give a call on the radio."

"Yes, sir. Understood."

"And, Hamfist," he said, "I'm really glad you're okay."

46

June 23, 1972

This was the ninth anniversary of the day I entered the Air Force Academy. It seemed a lifetime ago. So much had transpired in the intervening time. I'd gotten my degree. I'd been trained as a pilot. I'd flown in combat. I'd lost friends. I'd been shot down, twice. I'd fallen in love. And I'd gotten married.

When I was in my first week at the Academy, my squadron's Air Officer Commanding, Major Swain, interviewed each new cadet and asked each of us what our career ambitions were.

"Sir, I want to be a fighter pilot," I responded, without hesitation.

At the time, I was a an immature kid, a "doolie" with a shaved head, who didn't even know one fighter aircraft from another. And now, I was a fighter pilot. And I was a River Rat. The stars had aligned correctly.

I now had another ambition. Actually, two. I wanted to complete the magic 100 missions over North Vietnam. And I wanted to bag a MiG.

A few weeks after Operation Linebacker started, guys started showing up with 100-mission patches. These were guys on their second tours, who had already completed perhaps 80 or 90 missions over the north on their previous tours a few years earlier, before flying north of the DMZ had ended.

In the old days, when operations were still in effect over North Vietnam, during Operation Rolling Thunder, a pilot would be sent home after either completing 100 missions over the north or after being in theater for one year. With aggressive scheduling, a guy could DEROS home after six or seven months.

Now, all tours of duty were for one year, regardless of number of missions. I wasn't trying to get 100 missions over the north just to get sent home early, though that would have been nice. I wanted to get 100 missions because it was a milestone I had coveted ever since seeing the motivational movie, "There Is A Way" when I was in UPT. It was a merit badge for grown up boy scouts.

And I wanted a MiG, because shooting down enemy airplanes is what fighter pilots do. Truth be known, I wanted to be an ace, a fighter pilot with five aerial kills to his credit, like Colonel Ryan, my DO from pilot training. But getting one MiG would be a good start.

On this day, I stopped by Wing Intel for some pre-mission target study before our Special. As I was reviewing our mission briefing package, I was approached by Major Rover, the head of the Wolf FAC unit.

"Sorry to interrupt you, Hamfist. You have time for a short chat?"

"Sure thing, sir."

"Hamfist, I know you had some FAC

experience on your previous tour, and I wanted to see if you're interested in becoming a fast FAC. As you know, we lost Captain Sampson and Captain Garner last month, and two of our other Wolf FACs are going to DEROS in another month, so we have some openings, if you're interested."

I was flattered, really flattered. The Wolf FAC operation was highly selective, and it was a real honor to be invited to apply. And the Area of Operations for the Wolf FACs was the southern portion of North Vietnam, so getting 100 missions over the north would be a slam-dunk.

But the Wolf FAC AO was primarily in Route Pack One. And, I know this sounds stupid, there weren't many MiGs in Pack One. The MiGs were in Pack Six, Hanoi. If I became a Wolf FAC, I'd have less chance of bagging a MiG.

"I'm very honored that you've asked me, sir.

If it's okay with you, I'd like to think it over for a few days."

"Sure, no problem."

"Thank you, sir."

I already knew what my answer would be, but I wanted to think of a gracious way to bow out without sounding like an ungrateful jerk.

Our mission on this day was a strike on Kep airfield, northeast of Hanoi. Our route took us east over DaNang, then north over the water for refueling on Purple anchor.

While we were flying alongside the tanker, between top-off hookups, I loosened the leg straps of my parachute harness so I could unzip my flight suit from the bottom to use my piddle pack.

That was pretty much my standard operating procedure on the way to the target. While we were in formation with the tanker I would give the airplane to the WSO to let him get some stick time, and I'd chew an entire pack of Rolaids, drink most of the water in my canteen, and take a leak. Giving stick time to the back-seater was like having a great insurance policy. In the past, there had been more than one occasion when a back-seater had needed to land the airplane when the front-seat pilot had been incapacitated.

We ingressed the target area and set up a wheel pattern around Kep. Lead illuminated the target while we each rolled in separately and dropped our LGBs. We set up for 45-degree dive deliveries.

I rolled in from the north, dropped my bombs and transmitted, "Pickle, pickle, pickle". Then I executed a brisk 4-G pull-up.

Suddenly, I had an excruciating pain in my testicles. My first reaction was, "I've been shot in the balls!". Then I realized, I hadn't been hit. I had forgotten to tighten the leg straps of my parachute harness, and my body had shifted to the point that my testicles were caught between the my body and the harness.

And now my balls were being squeezed by four times my body weight. Six hundred-plus pounds of pressure on your nuts will get your attention real quick. As soon as I realized what the problem was, I pushed forward on the stick to ease off the Gs, and saw Mother Vietnam rushing toward me at 500 knots. I had no choice but to pull again, crushed nuts be damned.

I was in agony the whole flight back, and immediately went to see Dr. Myers, the Flight Surgeon, as soon as I landed.

"Drop your shorts and let me take a look," he said.

I gingerly lowered my shorts and looked down. I wasn't sure which one of us was more surprised. My testicles were swollen to the size of oranges.

"I've always heard that you fighter pilots had

big ones, but this is a first for me."

"I guess I'll be DNIF for a while."

Duty Not Involving Flying meant I wouldn't be able to fly for a while, but could perform other squadron duties.

"No way, Hamfist. You're totally grounded for five days. I want you to stay in your room, no duty, total bed rest. Off your feet completely."

"Since this happened on a combat mission," he said, "I'll be putting you in for a Purple Heart."

"If it's all the same to you, Doc, I'll pass on the Purple Heart. I already have one anyway."

"Okay, your call."

I'd already stood in front of large groups of people and received awards. The last thing I wanted was to be paraded in front of dozens of my peers while someone read a citation, "On that day, Captain Hancock had his balls crushed through mismanagement of his life support equipment”. No thanks!

47

Jun 29, 1972

I was back flying, off grounded status. We were scheduled for another Pack 6 mission to one of the Vu Chua railroad bridges. As we sat in the briefing room, a groan went up from the 130 or so pilots when we saw the Intel photo of the bridge.

"Your target today is the Vu Chua South railroad bridge," the Intel Officer intoned.

We had been on this miniscule bridge perhaps a dozen times already. We called it the "nitnoy bridge". Nitnoy was the Thai word for small. Interestingly, no one would own up to how he had learned the translation of that word, but we all picked up the term pretty quickly.

Every time we attacked the bridge, we knocked it down. And the gomers managed to rebuild it in a day or so. One of the pilots in another squadron, in frustration, wrote to his congressman, complaining that we were attacking small, insignificant bridges, like the Vu Chua bridge, "seven meters wide by 40 meters long, wood and steel construction". It just didn't make sense.

The letter to the congressman worked. Within a few days, the Rules of Engagement changed. "Effective immediately," the notice read, "no bridges shorter than 50 meters will be targeted during Operation Linebacker." We all reveled in the knowledge that the system worked. We would no longer be risking our lives to knock down an easily-repaired target.

And now, we once again saw the Vu Chua railroad bridge as our primary target.

"Your target today," declared the Intel Officer, "is the Vu Chua South railroad bridge, ten meters by seventy meters, wood and steel construction."

It was the same fucking bridge! The Seventh

Air Force planners had simply designated the approaches to the bridge as part of the overall length, and fudged the width. The bridge hadn't gotten any longer, they just *called* it longer to keep it on the target list.

We were all in a sour mood as we returned from Wing Headquarters to our squadron briefing room. To make matters worse, one of the eight crewmembers in our flight, Maple Flight, was Major Waller. He was going to be Maple two.

Major Waller had arrived at Ubon the day Linebacker started, May 10th. He was a highly experienced F-4 pilot. In fact, he had been flying the F-4 almost since its introduction into the Air Force inventory. He had over 3000 hours of F-4 time, all of it in Europe and the States. That was an incredible amount of experience. There were probably less than a dozen pilots in the Air Force with that much F-4 time. We all had really high hopes for him.

Unfortunately, he let us down. Although Major Waller was an incredibly experienced pilot, he was either very unlucky or had a fear of combat. Here we were, two months into Operation Linebacker, and he had not yet been to Hanoi.

He had been scheduled dozens of times, but something always seemed to happen to his aircraft that prevented him from making it to the target. There were at least ten times he ground aborted and didn't take off with the strike formation, and an equal number of times he air aborted. Every one of those times, one of our other squadron pilots had to fill in for him.

Major Waller quickly earned the nickname King. He thought it was an homage to his high fighter time. In actuality, it was a short form for “hangar king”, the masculine form of “hangar queen”, a term for an airplane that never flies due to excesive maintenance issues.

On this mission, Lieutenant Colonel Wiley,

our Squadron Commander and flight lead, gave a very short preflight briefing. Instead of the normal 45-minute mission briefing, Lieutenant Colonel Wiley kept it short.

"You all have the line-up cards, with takeoff times, tail numbers and frequencies. You already know the target. We will check in on Ground Control frequency at the scheduled time and taxi together to the arming area. Now Major Waller and I will go out and preflight his airplane. Any questions?"

We were all shocked. And elated. Finally King was going to go into combat!

My back-seater and I went out to the airplane at the usual time, did a thorough preflight, and carefully checked our bombs, two Mark-84Ls. The Mark-84 was a 2000-pound bomb, and the suffix L designated it as a laser-guided munition. As long as we had a laser to light up the target, these babies were going to hit it.

We cranked up at the appointed time, and I listened up on Ground frequency.

“Maple flight, check.”

“Two.”

“Three.”

“Four.” I was in the number four position.

So far so good. King's airplane hadn't broken yet. We taxied out in formation and pulled into the Arming Area, just short of the runway. A Maintenance Sergeant did a quick walk-around of each aircraft, to look for any obvious problems, such as hydraulic leaks. Then the Arming Crew pulled the pins on our bombs and we were armed.

We taxied onto the runway and took off, 15-second spacing. Join-up was uneventful, and we headed out to the refueling track. We hadn't been airborne twenty minutes when King tried to air abort.

“Maple Lead, this is Two. Let's go blankets.”

Blankets was the name of our squadron common frequency, UHF 234.5.

“Negative, Two,” lead responded. “We're staying on this frequency.”

“Maple Lead, this is Two. My abba-jabba seven has tumbled.”

The AJB-3/AJB-7 attitude reference on the F-4 was called the “abba-jabba seven”. It was an essential instrument for aircraft flight in instrument conditions. Today the weather was clear, and all of our bombs would be dropped in formation with the lead aircraft.

“Maple Two, this is Lead. Just put the light on the star and you'll do fine.”

Putting the “light on the star” was short-hand for lining up the wingtip light of the lead airplane with the star painted on his fuselage, which would put the wingman in proper close formation, with three feet wingtip separation. In other words, *just fly formation, Maple Two, and you won't need a goddam attitude indicator.*

The Major didn't want to give up without a fight.

"Maple Lead, I really think I should air abort."

"Light on the star, Two, and maintain radio silence."

As luck would have it, the weather ship that was sent to the target area an hour ahead of us had bad news. The entire Hanoi area was undercast, and we would not be able to attack. The primary mission was a weather cancel, and we all ended up diverting to different targets in Laos as single ships. And Maple Two got his wish – without an attitude reference he couldn't drop his bombs, so he returned to base unexpended. Another mission he didn't complete.

Our target was in NKP's Area of Operations. We made our rendezvous with our FAC, Nail 56. He was in an OV-10, and was a Pave Nail, which meant he had laser illumination gear onboard.

Apparently Nail 56 had already put in quite a few airstrikes. He was totally out of willie pete rockets.

"Maple four," he transmitted, "do you have me in sight?"

He was just to the north of me, at about 8000 feet, headed east.

"Affirmative," I answered.

"Okay, off my left wing is a river. You'll notice a bend in the river that looks like a set of tits. The target is in the cleavage. Just aim for the cleavage and I'll guide the bombs the rest of the way. I want you to make your run-in from south to north, with a break to the east. You're cleared in hot."

I was in position to make an immediate run-in, and pulled up for a high release. To get the bombs to guide properly, they needed to be released from 20,000 feet, with a ton of smash, preferably 500 knots. That meant I needed to pull up to well above 25,000 feet.

I kept the tits in sight as I pulled up high, rolled into a 120-degree bank and pulled my nose through into a 30-degree dive. The pipper was tracking perfectly to the cleavage. I reached 500 knots right at 20,000 feet, with the pipper directly on target. I was using a ballistic mills setting, which meant that even if there was a laser failure, I would have a good bomb. It might not be perfect, but a 2000-pound bomb can do a lot of damage even if it's not a direct hit. I pressed the pickle button, the bomb release button on the hand grip of the control stick.

“Pickle, pickle, pickle,” I transmitted. That was the signal for Nail 56 to turn on his laser.

I pulled off to the right, then banked left and looked at the target to see my bomb impact. Nothing. Not a ripple in the water. Not a kick-up of dust. Nothing. What could have happened?

"Awesome bomb! Great job, Maple!" yelled the FAC.

I looked back at the target, and still didn't see anything. Then I looked further to the north, probably two klicks or more, a full mile, and saw where the bomb had hit. It had impacted at the cleavage of another river that looked like tits. The 20,000-foot release, the 500 knots, and the good laser illumination had dragged my bomb all the way to the correct target. A full mile away.

On that mission I learned that a lot of smash and altitude on a laser guided bomb is like money in the bank.

And I also learned that, when you've been away from home long enough, *every* bend in the river looks like tits.

48

July 2, 1972

After the flight on June 29th, Lieutenant Colonel Wiley had gone over to Major Waller's airplane, which had landed an hour earlier. He'd climbed up into the cockpit and looked around.

The circuit breaker for the attitude indicator was popped – or pulled. He put power on the airplane and reset the circuit breaker, and the attitude indicator immediately erected. It seemed pretty clear that Major Waller had pulled the circuit breaker to give himself an air abort. But Lieutenant Colonel Wiley didn't immediately take any action.

He coordinated with the Maintenance folks to make sure he, Lieutenant Colonel Wiley, was assigned the same aircraft for the next two days. He wanted to personally fly it to see if the attitude indicator circuit breaker would pop.

It didn't.

For over a week there had been a request by Seventh Air Force, sent to every squadron, for a field grade officer to serve at Headquarters in Saigon, to help run the war as a staff officer. Every Squadron Commander had the same quandary. Should we send Seventh Air Force a really great pilot, who knew the targets and tactics? A great, experienced pilot could really help the war effort. But, at the same time, that same great pilot would be an incredible asset to the squadron mission. Maybe provide the kind of on-scene leadership that would save lives in combat.

In the end, it wasn't a tough choice at all for our Squadron Commander. Major Waller was not only *not* a combat asset to our squadron, he was an impediment. He counted against the squadron's manning level, but he didn't fly combat missions. That meant that every other pilot had to fly more combat missions, to pick up his slack.

Within a week, Major Waller was on his way to Saigon to serve on the Seventh Air Force staff. The irony wasn't lost on any of us. He would be in a staff job, would probably have lots of visibility with senior officers, and would probably make Lieutenant Colonel below the zone.

It was just like what Miles Miller had mentioned a few years earlier at DaNang, when Numb-nuts had gotten promoted: fuck up and move up.

49

July 3, 1972

Another day, another Special. This was going to be my 29th mission over the North, and I was starting to feel comfortable over Route Pack Six. Okay, not really comfortable. Probably a bit less scared.

Every Special was an 0400 brief for a dawn launch, and I had developed a kind of ritual. I woke up at 0230 and went to the O'Club for breakfast. Then I walked the half mile to Wing Headquarters, to look at the shoot-down board and read any messages in the Flight Crew Information File.

The FCIF was a large book with current must-read information, such as changes to Rules of Engagement. Back at the squadron there was a vertical card file, kind of like the time-card files you see at factories where workers grab their time cards to punch in and out of work. We each had an FCIF card, and every time there was a new FCIF item, we would date and initial the FCIF item number on our cards. That way, the squadron could document that we had all had each seen important, timely information before we flew.

Besides the FCIF, one of the things we each looked at in Intel was the shoot-down board. The board was a large white chart, probably about two feet wide by three feet high, with about twenty horizontal lines and about six vertical columns. The columns were labeled: Date, Call Sign, Type Aircraft, Location, Cause, and Results. The board was covered with Plexiglas.

Whenever a friendly aircraft went down, the information was filled in with grease pencil. It typically took several days for the board to fill up, and then the oldest information would be replaced by newer information. For example, if an F-4 was shot down a few days ago, we would all know his call sign in case he came up on

Guard frequency on his survival radio. There was about two weeks' worth of shoot-down information on the board. About half of the entries had “Rescued” in the Results column. Good old Jolly Greens.

After spending some time at Intel, I went to the Wing Briefing Room and waited for the mass briefing that would be held before we would return to our squadrons for individual flight briefings. Typically, all of our flights would be highly choreographed enterprises. Each flight had a very specific TOT – Time Over Target – and run-in direction. With sixteen four-ship flights of attack aircraft, it was essential for everyone to religiously stick to the script.

Our target was Kep Airfield, north of Hanoi. Our call sign was Brushy Flight. I was, again, number four in the formation.

Our route to the target was going to be via right turns. North over Laos, refueling along

Green anchor. Then a turn to the east over Thud Ridge, straight run-in to Kep, roll-in on the target in close fingertip formation, drop the bombs when lead pickled. Egress to the east over Haiphong, get feet wet and refuel over the South China Sea headed south. After refueling, we'd continue south until DaNang, then head west to Ubon.

It was going to be a pretty long mission, and I put three piddle packs in my helmet bag, since the F-4 had no relief tube. The piddle pack was a large plastic bag with a sponge inside, and was used as a portable urinal. The only way I wanted to be "feet wet" was when we egressed over the water.

We had a standard briefing, and again carried two Mark-84L bombs. Our flight was the fifth four-ship to depart Ubon during the mass launch. Takeoff and rejoin were normal.

When we reached Green anchor, we joined up with our tanker and each hooked up to refuel to tanks full. Then we flew in formation with the tanker as he headed north, and we periodically topped off the tanks, to be as full as possible at the drop-off point, just short of Thud Ridge. All of the refueling was accomplished in total radio silence.

It was quiet, but it was not uneventful. The boom operator in the tanker had the complex job of "threading the needle" to guide the refueling receptacle to our aircraft as we maneuvered the last several feet for the hookup. His duty station in the KC-135 tanker aircraft was in the tail of the aircraft, laying on his stomach and looking through a large window-like viewing port to guide the boom. It always impressed me that we could be executing this complex aerial ballet at over 300 knots, and it all worked flawlessly.

Our boomer on this flight wanted to give us a little comic relief and variety. Right as I hooked up for one of my final refueling hookups, I looked up at the boomer, about fifteen feet above me. In his window, he was holding up a centerfold from what was euphemistically called a "men's magazine". Actually, it was not the typical Playboy centerfold. It was much more graphic. I suspect he had gotten it at one of the overseas bases. His stunt made it a bit more challenging to maintain refueling position. And it sure broke up the monotony.

We had very little enemy reaction on the way in to the target. There were a few strobes on my RHAW gear – the Radar Homing And Warning system – but no SAMs. As we rolled in for the delivery, a lot of triple-A opened up on us. A lot.

We were in close fingertip formation, and as we were in a 120-degree bank we were engulfed by 37 mike mike airbursts. They looked like instantaneous dandelions blossoming in the air around our aircraft. I kept the light on the star as we rolled in, and no one in the flight broke formation. We rolled out on final, and lead called the bomb release.

“Three, two, one, pickle, pickle, pickle.”

We all pickled off our bombs, all of them, and they all guided to the target on the illumination from lead's laser. We put gigantic craters dead center in the runway.

As soon as we egressed the target area to the east, lead wagged his tail, signaling for us to go into spread tactical formation, 500 feet spacing between elements. Lead and two would be in fingertip formation, and number three and I would be in fingertip position 500 feet away, line abreast. This was determined to be the most effective formation for spotting MiGs and SAMs.

My head was on a swivel, looking for threats. Suddenly, number three, my element lead, spotted a SAM.

“SAM, SAM, left seven o'clock!”

There was no indication on my RHAW gear,

and it was clear this was no ordinary SAM. Typically, a normal SA-2 SAM launch is indicated by a RHAW gear warning, a green strobe appearing on the circular scope in the cockpit, indicating the direction of the threat and the intensity of the radar. It was possible, of course, for a SAM to be guided optically, without radar, so that it would not trigger our RHAW gear. But most SA-2s used radar and were flown in lead pursuit.

Lead pursuit was a flight path that pointed the SAM ahead of the target aircraft, intending for the supersonic SAM to meet up with the target aircraft at some point in front of the target's current position. It wasn't all that hard to defeat a lead pursuit SAM, if you saw it in time.

To defeat a lead pursuit SAM, you enter a shallow dive and pick up speed. The SAM will project your future position and head for a lower altitude, further out in front of your airplane. Then, when the SAM looks the size of a telephone pole, you pull up, hard, perhaps five or six G's. Immediately, your flight vector is in a totally different direction, and for the SAM to travel to a point now ahead of your airplane it would need to make a huge directional change, perhaps a 20-G pull. The SAM can't make that kind of turn, and it misses. It may detonate as a proximity burst, but it won't be a direct hit.

This SAM was different. It was flying lag pursuit, aiming directly at our aircraft. Much harder to defeat. It was holding steady at our left seven o'clock. It looked like it was attached to the rear of our airplanes by a long cable that was getting ever shorter.

During the target egress, my element was to the left of lead, and I was on the left side of my element lead. That put me closest to the incoming SAM. The first thing my element lead did was increase our spacing on lead's element. This way we could see which element was the target. We increased spacing to about 1500 feet, and all four aircraft started a shallow dive.

The SAM stayed with my element, pointing directly at us, closing rapidly. I stayed in fingertip formation, and kept watching the SAM in the rear-view mirror on the left side of the canopy bow. I had a really uncomfortable, familiar feeling. This SAM was going to get both of us.

As it disappeared from view in the mirror, blocked from view by my fuselage, I broke hard left. At least one of us was going to get hit. Maybe one of us wouldn't.

50

July 3, 1972

The SAM exploded directly alongside Number Three. It was close enough to shake my airplane, and loud enough for me to hear.

I quickly checked my telelight panel. There were no warning lights. My element lead, Number Three, was amazingly still flying, but had dozens of holes in his aircraft. The plane was pissing fuel, oil and hydraulic fluid all over the sky, making a white mist as the liquids vaporized into the thin air.

We continued heading east to get feet wet, and stayed in spread formation once we were over Haiphong Harbor. Lead came up on the radio.

"Four, give Three a damage check."

"Roger."

I maneuvered my airplane under Number

Three, and around each side of him.

"Number Three is losing a lot of fluids from numerous holes. No fires," I said.

"Be advised," number three transmitted, "Brushy Three has lost the Utility Hydraulic System."

The Utility Hydraulic System powered the refueling door that opened the hatch on top of the aircraft to allow the aerial refueling boom to connect to the aircraft. Without being able to open the refueling door, Number Three would not be able to refuel. He would need to land, quickly, before he lost all of his remaining fuel.

"Brushy Three," lead transmitted, "you are cleared out of the formation to RTB to DaNang. Brushy Four will escort you."

DaNang was the closest friendly base that could handle an F-4. I checked my fuel gauges, and I could see there was no problem for me to make it to DaNang without air-to-air refueling. The big question was: with fuel pissing out of his aircraft continuously, could Brushy Three make it?

51

July 3, 1972

I was really worried about Number Three making it to DaNang. He was still leaking fluids, although at a slower rate than earlier.

Brushy Three was leading our two-ship formation, and sounded totally calm on the radio. We went to post-strike frequency, then went over to DaNang Approach frequency, and he declared a fuel emergency and advised them that he would need to make an Approach End Barrier Engagement. He would need to do an AEBE because his hydraulic system was totally shot, so he would have no nose wheel steering or brakes. And, of course, with no Utility Hydraulic System, his engine would auto-accelerate once he was on the ground.

I flew chase position on Brushy Three all the way down final approach. Because of his loss of hydraulics, he had to make a no-flap approach, and had to blow his landing gear down with the emergency pneumatic system. He made a perfect landing and AEBE on Runway 35 Right. I executed a go-around and pulled a left closed pattern for the only open runway, Runway 35 Left.

As I turned final, I performed one last fuel check and saw that I was really tight on fuel. I was totally amazed that Brushy Three had made it all the way to DaNang, considering the damage his airplane had sustained.

After I landed, my WSO, Cat Katlin, and I went to the Intel debriefing room, then met up with the crew of Brushy Three at the Crew Break Room. They looked relieved. Really relieved.

The Crew Break Room had sandwiches, drinks and dessert set out on a large table, and on one side of the room were the typical flight planning charts and documents normally found at Base Ops. There was a Major in charge of the operation, and he advised me that my aircraft was being refueled and would be available for a flight back to Ubon whenever I was ready. And he told me I would be leading a two-ship flight.

Since I was not officially designated a Flight Lead, I was a bit puzzled.

"I'll be your wingman today."

I turned around to see who was talking to me, and saw a tall Major.

"I'm Dick Handler," he said, holding out his hand.

"Pleased to meet you, sir." I wasn't about to ask him how he got that nickname. "I'm Hamfist Hancock. I'm glad to be the lead, sir, but how come you're not flying lead today?"

"I'm going to be solo. So it will be easier all around if you lead. Let's head out to the airplanes, and I'll show you why I'm solo."

We finished our sandwiches, and headed out

to the flight line. The Major's plane was in the revetment next to mine. We went over to his bird.

"That's my battle damage," he remarked, pointing to a small hole in the rear canopy. "I can't fully pressurize, so we'll have to stay below 20,000 feet."

"No problem, sir. What happened to your back-seater?" I had the sick feeling in the pit of my stomach that I already knew the answer.

"We were putting in a string of sensors for Igloo White, ingressing the target area on the deck, perhaps 30 feet above the ground. We were going fast, close to supersonic, jinking all the time. There was no way anyone could track us with ground fire."

"Right after our release, I heard a small arms round hit our aircraft, and then I couldn't hear my WSO on hot mike. At first I thought maybe we had taken a hit that damaged our interphone, but I declared an emergency and

RTB'd to DaNang as fast as I could. I asked for an ambulance to meet the aircraft, and I shut down as soon as I exited the runway."

"It turned out the small arms round was my WSO's golden BB," he continued. "It got him right through the heart."

He seemed to be having a hard time holding back tears.

"Are you okay to fly, sir?" I asked.

"Yeah, I'll be okay, as long as you lead, and all I need to do is put the light on the star."

"You got it, sir. We'll check in on Ground frequency in five minutes."

During my previous tour at DaNang, and on this tour at Ubon, we had often talked about the so-called "golden BB", the bullet with an your name on it, when your number is up. I used to make wise-ass jokes about it.

"Yeah, but what if my back-seater's number is up?"

Now I knew the answer.

52

July 4, 1972

We had a total of six AN/AVQ-10 Pave Knife pods at Ubon. These were really incredibly pieces of technology. The Pave Knife pod had a gyro-stabilized laser designator that allowed the WSO in the back seat of the lead airplane to illuminate the target while the aircraft was maneuvering. Even if the airplane temporarily blanked out the view of the target through its maneuvering, the cross-hairs on the WSO's scope would still be on the target when it came back into view.

The other way to illuminate the target with a guidance laser was with the Pave Way, also called the Zot Box. It was a hand-held device, about the size of a shoe box, that had a laser designator. The WSO would hold the Zot Box and keep it pointed at the target while the bombs fell. The Pave Nail FACs, in OV-10s, also used the Zot Box to designate targets.

Regardless of the laser designator in use, if the target was illuminated, the bombs would hit.

The Pave Knife pod looked a lot like an external fuel tank to someone not trained in aircraft recognition. Unless you knew exactly what to look for, you would be hard-pressed to know which F-4 had a Pave Knife pod.

On this day, although I wasn't flying, it became really clear to me that the bad guys had spies on the ground at Ubon. The lead aircraft of one of the flights from another squadron at Ubon was carrying a Pave Knife pod on a Pack Six mission.

His target was near Kep Airfield. As his flight entered the target area, more than a dozen SAMs were fired at his aircraft. Only at his aircraft.

He was hit and headed out to sea. Shortly after getting feet wet, he lost all of his hydraulics and his flight controls failed. He and his back-seater bailed out over the ocean and were fairly quickly picked up by a nearby Navy ship.

Now we only had five Pave Knife pods.

The next day there was a story circulating around Ubon – I don't know whether it was true or not – that Navy frogmen had been sent to the wreckage on the ocean floor, to recover sensitive electronics from the Pave Knife pod. When they found the wreckage, the story went, they got into an underwater engagement – dogfight – with Russian frogmen who had also been dispatched to get pieces of the pod.

It sure made a great story.

53

July 10, 1972

This was going to be a really great mission. Lieutenant Colonel Wiley was our flight lead, and we were fragged for a flight deep into North Vietnam to attack some bridges on the northwest railroad, a rail artery that ran from China to Hanoi. As usual, I was number four.

We were going to take off at maximum gross weight, with full fuel plus two Mark 84L 2000-pound bombs per airplane. With external fuel tanks plus the large frontal area of the bombs and our ever-present AIM-7 Sidewinder missiles, each airplane had a really high drag index. That, plus the high ambient temperature, meant we would use most of the available runway for the takeoff roll.

“If you don't fly your airplane exactly right on takeoff, you won't turn into a pumpkin,” quipped Lieutenant Colonel Wiley, “but you might turn into a marshmallow."

Lieutenant Colonel Wiley had a way of injecting a little humor into our briefings that helped dissipate our pre-launch jitters. We all laughed, nervous laughter, really. He was kidding, but he wasn't kidding.

After a thorough preflight briefing, we all headed to the latrine for that last, essential pit stop. The latrine in the squadron was a three-holer, not nearly sufficient for all the pilots to use for a pre-mission dump. As a result, every flight lead tried to finish his briefing as quickly as he could, so his pilots could get a good place in line for the latrine.

After that essential detour, I headed out ot my airplane with my WSO, Tommy Thompson. I preflighted the airplane while Tommy preflighted the bombs and missiles, and we strapped in. I checked my watch, and, at exactly the appointed time, we started engines.

We checked in on Ground frequency and

taxied in formation to the quick check/arming area. The Maintenance Sergeant checked over our airplanes and we were all good to go. Then the arming crew pulled our pins and it was our turn to take the runway.

The runway at Ubon was not level. There was an uphill slope at the beginning of the runway, and a downhill slope at the end. The middle of the runway was the high point, and it was a normal occurrence that an airplane on takeoff would disappear from view after cresting the hill at mid-field.

We lined up in trail formation on the runway and performed our pre-takeoff checks. Then Lead started rolling. I hacked my clock. We were using 15 second spacing for the takeoffs. Right as Number Two started rolling, Lead crested the hill at the midpoint of the runway and disappeared from view, out of sight on the last half of the runway. Fifteen seconds later, Number Two disappeared from sight over the hill and Number Three started his takeoff roll.

Just as Number Three started rolling, Number Two came on the radio.

“Abort, abort, abort! Maple Lead has aborted and is on fire. Two is aborting.”

“Maple Three, abort, abort, abort.”

I echoed the call. “Maple Four, abort, abort, abort.”

Number Three was stopped on the runway ahead of me, and I held my position. Somewhere, out of view, were Maple Lead and Maple Two. Then I saw the smoke rising from the far end of the runway. And then, after about five minutes, came the explosions.

First, the ejection seats cooked off. Then, the 2000-pound bombs exploded, both of them, along with the AIM-7s. Finally, a massive conflagration engulfed Lead's airplane.

Ubon had only one runway, and had a curved taxiway that could not be used for takeoffs or landings. The field was closed, and our mission was cancelled. It took about 45 minutes to de-conflict ground traffic and get all of the airplanes recovered to their revetments. During the whole time, none of us knew the status of the crew of Maple Lead.

As it turned out, Lieutenant Colonel Wiley had been prescient. At precisely the worst possible time on takeoff, his left main landing gear tire disintegrated. He was doing 165 knots, too slow to fly, too damned fast to abort without using the departure end barrier.

He lowered his tail hook and snagged the barrier, but shrapnel from the burst tire had punctured his wing fuel tank, and the left side of his aircraft caught fire. While he shut down the engines, his WSO, Zoomie Powell, unstrapped and went out of the plane over the right side. Zoomie quickly ran the hundred or so yards to a drainage ditch, and hunkered down.

Zoomie was a small, wiry Second

Lieutenant, a 1970 graduate of the Air Force Academy. He had bad eyes, and couldn't get into pilot training, so he became a navigator. He was at the top of his Nav class, and scored an F-4 back seat assignment. He'd arrived at Ubon about the same time I did. When Zoomie looked back from the ditch, he expected to see Lieutenant Colonel Wiley close on his tail.

Instead, Lieutenant Colonel Wiley was still in the cockpit. His leg restraint release hadn't worked, and he had to carefully disconnect each restraint separately. Left lower leg restraint. Left upper leg restraint. Right lower leg restraint. Right upper leg restraint. Harness release. All this time, his raised canopy was melting around him, dripping burning Plexiglas onto his nomex flight suit.

When Zoomie saw Lieutenant Colonel Wiley hung up in the cockpit, he sprinted back to the burning aircraft, and climbed up the right side to help Wiley get out. He pulled the harness release just as Lieutenant Colonel Wiley finally got free of the leg restraints, and he pulled Wiley out of the cockpit.

They both tumbled to the tarmac, and Lieutenant Colonel Wiley broke his heel. Zoomie picked him up and carried him on his shoulder to the drainage ditch. They hunkered down just as the munitions started cooking off.

Walnut Lead's plane had carried one of the few remaining Pave Knife pods. It was destroyed, of course. Now there were only four AN/AVQ-10 Pave Knife pods left at Ubon.

Zoomie later received the Airman's Medal, one of the highest non-combat awards you can get.

Well deserved.

54

July 17, 1972

The Special this day was to a target northeast of Kep Airfield, some munitions storage. My WSO was Bob "Deacon" Diller, the same Bob Diller who had been my back-seater in RTU. Deacon had originally been assigned to DaNang, and then transferred to Ubon when operations at DaNang had drawn down.

Our call sign was Utah Flight, and I was, as usual, Number Four. Target ingress was fairly uneventful, with a few SAM indications on our RHAW gear, but no actual SAM sightings. We set up a wheel orbit over the target and rolled in individually while Lead illuminated the target. As I was rolling in, with a bank angle of 135 degrees, my G-suit ran away to full inflation.

The G-suit, also called "fast pants", is an elastic garment that is worn over the bottom half of the flight suit. There are inflatable rubber bladders around the upper legs and lower torso. These bladders inflate proportional to the G-loading on the aircraft, to prevent blood flow from pooling in the lower extremities. That way, under heavy G-loading, the G-suit helps keep blood flowing to the brain. Air from the aircraft pneumatic system inflates the G-suit to a lesser or greater degree, metered by the subsystem in the airplane that senses G-loading. The G-suit is pretty effective at helping the pilot tolerate heavy G-loads.

Unfortunately, in this particular case, the valve in the aircraft that controlled air to inflate the G-suit had malfunctioned. Under normal circumstances, all I would need to do to stop the erroneous inflation would be to disconnect the G-suit hose from the quick-release located on the left subpanel of the cockpit.

But this was not normal circumstances. I was close to upside down, trying to keep the target in sight while attempting to achieve perfect delivery parameters. Probably, a lot of jocks would have been able to simply reach down to the left side of the cockpit and release the G-suit connection. I was not one of those jocks. I needed to concentrate on the bomb delivery, G-suit runaway be damned. I would disconnect it after my pull off.

With the G-suit fully inflated, I felt like a giant python had wrapped around my body. I could hardly breathe. I tensed my abs and performed a Valsalva maneuver, trying to ignore the intense pressure, and completed the bomb delivery. Just as I pulled off the target, Deacon started screaming on the intercom.

"SAM,SAM, break right! Break right!"

I couldn't see the SAM, but when my WSO is screaming to break right, I break right. Normally, with a properly operating G-suit, I could sense the loading on the airplane. I knew what a 4-G pullout felt like. But with a fully inflated G-suit, everything felt different. I pulled on the pole with what I thought was the correct amount of pressure for a SAM break, and then, when the dust had settled, I reached down and disconnected the G-suit connector. The suit deflated and I could finally breathe.

“That was some pull-out,” Deacon commented.

“Yeah, the SAM didn't get us.”

I had assumed Deacon was remarking about the SAM threat. But he had been talking about the way I had just overstressed the aircraft.

“Look at the G-meter, Hamfist.”

“Holy shit! Nine point five G's! Are you okay, Deacon?”

“I'll live. But give me a heads-up next time you try to set a new record on G-loading.”

I had overstressed the aircraft. I flew it as gently as I could, and after we landed, we couldn't open our canopies. The canopy operation was controlled through the aircraft pneumatic system, and the excessive loading on the aircraft had ruptured the pneumatic accumulator.

Clearly, I had earned my nickname Hamfist. The aircraft had to undergo a major inspection to make sure I hadn't broken anything else.

Hamfist, indeed.

55

July 17, 1972

When I got back to the squadron, I expected to get a ration of shit from the rest of the guys in my flight for overstressing the aircraft. Instead, everybody was listening to the radio.

Jane Fonda had been visiting Hanoi, and was making radio broadcasts against our troops. We all listened in silent disgust as we bore witness to Treason being committed in real time.

"I don't know what your officers tell you, you are loading, those of you who load the bombs on the planes. But, one thing that you should know is that these weapons are illegal and that's not, that's not just rhetoric. They were outlawed, these kind of weapons, by several conventions of which the United States was a signatory -- two Hague conventions. And the use of these bombs or the condoning the use of these bombs makes one a war criminal."

"The men who are ordering you to use these weapons are war criminals according to international law, and in, in the past, in Germany and in Japan, men who were guilty of these kind of crimes were tried and executed."

Finally Major Moose Moore, one of the senior WSOs, went over to the radio and turned it off.

“I've heard enough,” he said.

Nobody objected. Now I knew how the GIs felt when they heard Tokyo Rose during World War Two. We had seen photos of Fonda in the Stars & Stripes, posing on a triple-A gun. For all we knew, she could have been doing some of the shooting at us.

Fighter pilots are a resourceful group. I don't know who did it, or how he did it, but the very next day there were decals with Jane Fonda's picture on them in every urinal on the entire base. Piss on Jane Fonda.

And we were all comforted by the knowledge, with certainty, that she would be charged and convicted of Treason when she returned to the States.

56

July 30, 1972

This mission was going to be a total goat-fuck. We had been fragged on the same target, northwest of Hanoi, for ten days. Every day, the mission was weather cancelled. Finally, the weather was good, and we were going to go.

What made the mission so incredibly bad was the route we were using. One of the geniuses at Seventh Air Force had gotten the bright idea that we needed to change our target ingress routes. We always attacked targets northwest of Hanoi by flying north over Laos and doing right turns, entering North Vietnam over Thud Ridge. We always attacked targets south and east of Hanoi by going north over the ocean and making left turns.

This time, the thinking went, we would ingress over the ocean and make left turns and attack targets northwest of Hanoi. The SAMs would all be pointing the wrong way! That brilliant idea had one major flaw: SAMs are not mounted in concrete, they are mobile. It takes, perhaps, three minutes to change a SAM from west-facing to east-facing.

Then there was the fact that the whole plan hadn't changed during the past ten days, and the spies at Ubon had undoubtedly heard about the mission. And, unfortunately, there were a lot of guys who didn't really pay a lot of attention to Operations Security. More than once I would be in the bar and hear, "We weather cancelled again on that stupid fucking mission that has us running in feet wet to attack a target north of Kep."

Finally, on the day of the strike, as we were on Purple refueling track on our way to the target, one of the tankers said, on strike frequency, "What time are you guys planning on tanker drop off for Kep?"

The only intelligent thing I heard was the response, from the lead of one of the strike flights.

"Subtract 12877 from your tail number for the drop-off time in zulu."

So, our plan had been compromised. That was evident as soon as we got over the land. We ingressed North Vietnam south of Hanoi, headed northwest. Before we even got west of Hanoi, we had dodged four SAMs. Another two SAMs over the target.

We made a left roll-in on target in close fingertip formation. I was, as usual, number four, on the right side of the formation. My WSO, Jinx Jenkins, was an FNG on his first Pack Six mission. As we rolled out for our delivery, I was pushing forward, pressed against my lap belt by negative-Gs. Dust and debris from the cockpit floor floated up and got into my eyes.

I blinked hard several times and cleared my

vision. I saw that I was getting close, too close, to Number Three, probably only about one foot of spacing. I banked away from Three, and ended up even closer. It hadn't occurred to me until just then that, with negative Gs, I would need to bank *toward* Three to increase my distance. It wasn't something that was intuitively obvious to me.

We all pickled in unison and lead illuminated the target for a direct hit. As we pulled off target, Lead switched us over to post-strike frequency and called for a fuel check.

As soon as I checked my fuel gauges, I knew I was in deep shit. I had less than half the fuel of the other planes in our flight. Something was wrong. Terribly wrong.

We got feet wet and performed another fuel check. Now I was down to less than 15 minutes of fuel. Our flight lead was new – on his first four-ship lead. And he was running out of ideas.

My element lead, Walnut Three, was Springs Springer. Springs came up on the radio.

"Walnut Lead, Three. Request permission to take the lead."

"Roger, Three," Lead answered, "You have the lead." To his credit, Walnut Lead didn't let his ego get in the way of saving my ass.

Three came up on the radio.

"Walnut flight go Guard."

"One."

"Two."

"Four."

We were now on Guard, the emergency frequency.

"Walnut flight check."

"One."

"Two."

"Four."

"Mayday, mayday, mayday. This is Walnut Three on Guard. We need an emergency tanker to Haiphong Harbor *now*!"

Almost immediately, we got a response.

"Purple two-eight's on the way."

"Roger, Purple 28, say your pigeons off Red Crown."

Red Crown was a Navy ship with a TACAN transmitter, that we used for navigation.

"Purple 28 is Red Crown 235 for 44."

Springs did some mental gymnastics and computed a point-to-point rendezvous heading for our flight and Purple 28. We made a slight heading correction to the left.

"Purple 28," Springs transmitted, "fly heading 340, and say your angels."

"Roger. Purple 28 at angels 30."

We were also at 30,000 feet. I could see Walnut Three's WSO hunched over his radar, looking for Purple 28.

"Purple 28, we have you on our radar. Start a left turn to a heading of south."

"Roger."

While all of this was going on, Jinx was reading our Preparation For Bailout checklist over the interphone.

"Lock shoulder harness."

"Locked."

"Tighten lap belt."

"Tightened."

"Insert oxygen mask bayonets to last locking position of helmet receiver."

"Inserted."

"Lower helmet visors and tighten chin strap."

"Done."

"Adjust sitting height as necessary."

"Adjusted."

"Stow all loose objects."

"Stowed."

I was operating on mental autopilot, and not doing too well. I was in what psychologists call "negative panic", sounding calm, cool and collected, but totally out to lunch. I had answered that I had stowed loose objects, but I still had my small camera hanging from my CRU-60/P oxygen connector. If I had bailed out, it would probably have inflicted serious injury to my head. But at least I sounded cool.

Walnut Three pointed at me and then pointed forward, giving me the lead.

"Purple 28, Walnut Three. Start a toboggan maneuver."

"Roger."

I looked ahead of the aircraft, and I was staring at the back end of a KC-135 tanker aircraft. I had been so head-up-and-locked that

I had been oblivious to the entire rendezvous.

"Walnut four," Three transmitted, "start a half nozzle descent."

"Roger."

I pulled the throttles back until the nozzle gauge indicated half open on each engine. That was the best endurance power setting for a glide.

I was now in the pre-contact position, flying downhill in a toboggan refueling, an emergency procedure designed exactly for my situation. A lot of pilots had demonstrated incredible airmanship to get me to this point. All I could think is, I sure don't want to live up to the name Hamfist and screw this up. I glanced at my fuel gauge. I had zero on the tape, and 0030 on the counter. That meant I had about two minutes fuel remaining. With the known tolerance in the fuel gauge, my fuel could have been a bit more, could have been even less.

I opened my refueling door and immediately

felt the comforting “clunk” of the boom seating into the receptacle. My fuel gauges started increasing immediately.

I wasn't going to bail out today.

57

July 31, 1972

For the past day I'd been trying to locate the Aircraft Commander of Purple 28. I knew that most of the Strategic Air Command tanker aircraft were based somewhere in Thailand. Since U-Tapao Air Base was a major SAC base, I looked there first.

I placed an autovon call to the U-Tapao O'Club. The Club Receptionist answered.

"Could you please page the Aircraft Commander from Purple 28?"

I waited. No one came to the phone. Then the Receptionist came back on the line.

"I'm sorry, sir, no one has answered."

"Okay. Please page any crew member from Purple 28."

Again, no answer.

“Please page any tanker crewmember.”

Finally, someone came on the line.

“Who is this, and what is it you want?”

“This is Captain Hamilton Hancock, and Purple 28 saved my ass yesterday. I'm trying to find out who he is, so I can properly thank him.”

“Oh. Look, this is SAC, so nobody ever answers the phone if they don't know who it is. It will most likely just be another shit detail.”

Finally, I was able to have a Captain-to-Captain talk with someone who could help me. It turned out Purple 28 was not based at U-Tapao, but I got the information I needed.

I made an appointment to see the Wing D.O., after getting clearance from the new Squadron Commander, Lieutenant Colonel Smith. The D.O. agreed to see me right away. I entered his office and saluted.

“Captain Hancock reporting, sir.”

"What can I do for you, Hamfist?"

"Sir, the crew of Purple 28 flew all the way up into Haiphong Harbor to save my ass two days ago, and I'd like to submit them for a medal."

"I'm ahead of you, Hamfist. As soon as I heard about your mission, I had my Admin guys get on it. We heard back from SAC Headquarters that they wanted to court-martial the crew for putting a valuable SAC resource into harm's way just to rescue one F-4."

"Just to rescue one F-4," he repeated. "Can you believe that? I have a call in to PACAF Headquarters. We'll let them fight it out, four-star to four-star. We'll get Purple 28 some kind of award. And not a court-martial."

"Thank you, sir."

"One last thing, Hamfist. We had your airplane checked out. Turns out your Variable Inlet Ramps were fully extended. They got a bad ramp signal from your ADC. It's fixed now."

"Thank you, sir."

I saluted, did a sharp about-face, and left the office.

The Air Data Computer was the brains of the airplane. Among other things, the ADC scheduled movement of the Variable Inlet Ramps at the inlets of the engines to optimize fuel efficiency and power. The ramps being extended, in the wrong position, had caused me to use more fuel than the other aircraft in my flight, more fuel than it should have used.

An errant electron had almost caused me to bail out.

58

August 1, 1972

Being based in Thailand was totally different from being based in Vietnam. In Vietnam, we couldn't go off base. In Vietnam, when we landed, the war just changed character; instead of being shot at in the air, we received rocket attacks and got shot at on the ground.

In Thailand, we could go off base, and we did all the time. We found people who smiled. When we landed, we were in a peaceful environment. No rocket attacks. Nobody shot at us once we landed. I often thought that the combat credit shouldn't have been the same for Thailand and Vietnam. But it was.

Lots of guys had their wives there to spend time with them. On their days off, they would take the train down to Bangkok and be in a modern city with great hotels, restaurants and clubs. If Sam had been a civilian, I could have brought her over.

But all was not roses. Relations were starting to get strained between the Thais and the guys on base. For one thing, a lot of the guys weren't very sensitive to the customs and culture of Thailand.

Two young Airmen were on their day off and rented bicycles, to see the countryside. At some point, out in the middle of nowhere, they came upon a giant statue of Buddha. They thought it would be nice to get photos of themselves with Buddha. Sitting in Buddha's upturned palm. They thought it was pretty cool.

Until they got their film developed.

They took their film to the local Thai Photo Shop, on base. When the Photo Shop developed the film, they were outraged that those foreigners had desecrated their religious symbol. They reported the offense to the local police, and the Airmen were immediately arrested.

It was a slam-dunk case, with incriminating photo evidence. The Airmen were sentenced to three years in a Thai prison. Fortunately for them, they were covered by the Status of Forces Agreement. This meant that base personnel would visit them weekly and bring books, magazines and American food to them. If and when the base ever closed, the Airmen would be transferred to American prisons to serve out the remainder of their sentences.

The Thai Photo Shop was a thorn in our sides for another reason. One of the pilots from another squadron had taken his camera on a mission over Pack Six, and had gotten a few really good aerial photos of downtown Hanoi. He left the film off at the Thai Photo Shop to be developed. When he went to pick up his pictures, he saw a giant enlargement of his photo for sale in the front window.

"I took that picture," he said.

"Yes. It good picture."

"That's my property. You can't sell it."

"We sell. Nothing you can do."

They were correct. Thailand did not subscribe to the International Copyright Convention. Intellectual property rights meant nothing to them. They could, and did, make copies of photos that were brought in for processing. It didn't take long for all of us to boycott the Thai Photo Shop and learn to process our own film at the base Photo Hobby Shop.

Then there was our relationship with the taxi drivers. Thai taxi cabs did not have meters. Normally, we would negotiate a fare in advance. Sometimes, guys who didn't know better would get into a taxi and then argue over the fare after they got to their destination.

That's what happened to an Airman who had only been on base about a week. He took a cab from a restaurant to the main gate of the base. When he arrived, he got into an argument with the driver. Finally, in total frustration, he threw a fist-full of *baht* at the driver.

“Here's your fucking money.”

Some of the money landed on the ground. The King's picture is on the money, and the King is sacred. The driver pulled out a knife and stabbed the Airman. Several times. Stabbed him dead.

The police were called, and, basically, congratulated the driver on his patriotic act. He had killed the foreigner who had desecrated the King's picture. Good for him.

Relations with the local Thais were at an all-time low. I almost never heard the word “Thai” without the prefix “fucking”. “The fucking Thais”.

On this day, we had another Special. Instead of LGBs, we were going to carry dumb bombs. And the Intel Officer didn't tell us what our target was, he merely told us the coordinates to enter into our LORAN bombing systems. In fact, he said, we would launch even if the target was covered by clouds. We would make straight-and-level bomb deliveries over a target in Pack Two.

To a man, we all demanded to know what the target was. Finally, he projected a photo of the target, a railroad yard. A railroad yard with no trains, just some railroad ties.

“Your target is some railroad supplies in a low-threat environment. We want to test the operation and accuracy of the LORAN bombing system over North Vietnam. Basically, you'll be bombing railroad ties.”

“We'll be bombing ties,” someone shouted from the back of the room. “Finally, we get to bomb the fucking Thais.”

The room erupted in laughter.

We all knew that the LORAN bombing system was incredibly accurate, when we used it in Laos and South Vietnam. We would make our bombing runs in wings-level flight. Any maneuvering would cause the system to lock up and give a “settle” light, which would require several seconds to disappear. The system didn't work if the settle light was illuminated.

The problem, besides the settle light, was that LORAN was only accurate when the signal lines from the various LORAN sites crossed at right angles, as they did in South Vietnam. Further north, in North Vietnam, the signal lines crossed at sharp angles, giving unpredictable results. Apparently, the planners at Seventh Air Force wanted to see how accurate our bombs would be if we used the LORAN bombing system over North Vietnam.

We all realized how ridiculous that was. Nobody flew wings level over Hanoi.

We had no idea how wrong we could be.

59

October 1, 1972

It seemed like I never got to go on the missions that really were interesting. I had been the ground spare and didn't launch when the Doumer Bridge was knocked down, the first day of Linebacker. It would have been great to have been on that strike. And I didn't fly on May 13th, the day our wing destroyed the Thanh Hoa Bridge. In 1965, thuds had flown 873 sorties, and lost 11 aircraft, trying to knock it down. And now that "indestructible" bridge had been dropped by one strike flight with smart bombs.

Then, on this day, there was a once-in-a-lifetime event the guys on the Special witnessed. They were attacking targets right downtown, and the enemy reaction was fierce. Triple-A so thick you could walk on it, and SAMs were being fired like they were going out of style.

And suddenly, all of the ground fire stopped. The war instantly came to a screeching halt. It was like in a sporting event where the referee has just blown the whistle.

One of the strike aircraft identified the reason for the interruption of hostilities.

“This is Maple One,” he transmitted on strike frequency, “Everyone hold high and dry. There's a Russian cargo plane on final to Gia Lam.”

The fighters stopped their deliveries and orbited the city, while the Antonov AN-12 made its approach and landing at the downtown civilian airport. The gomers didn't want to fire into the air for fear of inadvertently hitting the Russian plane. The strike aircraft didn't want to accidently hit the Russian plane and start a ground war at the United Nations. How the Russians could have sent a plane to Hanoi during an airstrike was anyone's guess. We always hit the targets at the same time, so whoever had scheduled the cargo flight was a complete idiot. Or, the Russians were looking to intentionally create an international incident.

So, like a basketball game where one side had called "Time Out", everyone stopped what they were doing, until the AN-12 had completed its landing. Then, just as suddenly, the war started again. MiGs reappeared, SAMs started launching again, and triple-A once again created an artificial overcast. And the strike aircraft once again made their runs.

Another really interesting thing happened during the Special this day. Some of the protection from MiGs was provided by Marine A-4s, call sign Bar Cap. On this day, Bar Cap One had gotten into an engagement with a MiG-21 and had fired his missile. Right after his weapons release, before his missile had time to hit the MiG, a camouflaged MiG-17 came up from behind him and shot him down.

He successfully bailed out, and, while he was in the chute, he came up on his survival radio.

When an Air force pilot gets shot down and gets on the radio, the typical transmission is something like, “Mayday, Mayday, Mayday. Maple One Alpha has a good chute, launch the SAR”. This Marine was different.

“This is Bar Cap One. I have a good chute. Now someone come up on guard and tell me if I got that sonofabitch!”

When I heard that story, it became clear to me that if another Marine got shot down on the other side of Hanoi, we'd have the gomers surrounded!

60

October 2, 1972

Although this mission, my sixty-second Counter, was deep into North Vietnam, it was not a Special. It was a dumb bomb mission to attack an enemy barracks complex at Dien Bien Phu.

Dien Bien Phu was historically significant, as it was the location of the resounding French defeat in 1954 that ended the French dominance in Indochina. The North Vietnamese military commander who orchestrated the defeat of the French was General Vo Nguyen Giap. Giap was a brilliant military strategist, and now, eighteen years later, he was still in command of the North Vietnamese military.

We may have been too late to help the French, but we were going to kick ass on this mission. Our call sign was Beech, and, as usual,

I was Number Four.

Our bomb load was six Mk-82s and four Mk-83s on each aircraft. This was my first time carrying Mk-83s, at 1000 pounds each. I'd carried 500-pound Mk-82s scores of times, as well as 2000-pound Mk-84s. From a weapons delivery perspective, there wasn't much difference between dropping one bomb versus another, other than the different mill setting and the slight difference in the way the airplane shuddered when the bombs came off.

As the fourth member of the flight, I was the last to roll in on the target. The previous aircraft in the flight had all bracketed the target pretty well, but no cigar. I rolled in, made a slight adjustment to the offset aim point based on the speed and direction of the blowing smoke from the previous hits, and pickled off my bombs. Then I pulled off and banked sharply to the left to see my results.

The target was gone, obliterated by my

perfect, absolutely perfect, bombs. I had forgotten how rewarding it was to drop dumb bombs, after back-to-back missions dropping smart bombs. Anybody can drop perfect smart bombs, as long as the laser is working. I proved that at Tits River. But when you release dumb bombs and score a perfect shack, now *that's* rewarding.

The French should have called for assistance from Beech Flight back in 1954.

61

October 23, 1972

In her typical fashion, Sam had managed to get a TDY assignment to Ubon for almost a month. She had been with me for the past 27 days.

A lot of the guys had their wives with them at Ubon. There were so many that, at one of the squadron parties, someone had quipped that it looked like a meeting of the Officer's Wives Club. Some of the guys actually had their wives staying with them in the hootch. Since we always shared a room with another pilot, that usually didn't work out too well.

The way most guys worked it when their wives came to town was to get rooms at the Ubol Hotel, in downtown Ubon Rachathani. So that's where we stayed while Sam was at Ubon.

The hotel was okay. Nothing fancy, a bedroom and bathroom. A cold tile floor. Just someplace we could have a little privacy. The water at the hotel was local water, not really safe for drinking, so we would fill empty whiskey bottles with drinking water on base, and bring them back to the hotel with us each night.

One time, when a hotel employee saw us carrying the water bottles, she said, “No need bring water. I fill for you.” So I gave her one of the empty bottles. I assumed – I forgot, it's not smart to assume – that she would fill the bottle from some source of clean drinking water. When she brought the bottle back to me, I thanked her and gave her a small tip.

Then I held the bottle up to the light. As I squinted at the bottle, I saw thin, thread-like worms everywhere in the water. If we had taken a drink from that bottle, we would have gotten parasites that could have caused serious illness. We learned our lesson. Only base water.

Besides wives, some of the guys had local

girlfriends, called *tilots*. Basically, the guy would financially support his *tilot*, and she would be monogamous with him the whole time he was at Ubon. She would be exclusive, his local wife. When he DEROSed, his *tilot* would be back on the market.

There was a story, probably total bullshit, that the wife of one of the guys had visited him at Ubon and had found out that he had a *tilot*. Naturally, in wifely fashion, she wanted to see what her husband's *tilot* looked like.

"I'll tell you what I'll do," he said to his wife, "We'll go to the club downtown where I usually meet with my *tilot*, and you will get a chance to see her."

So, the guy and his wife went to the club downtown. While the wife waited by the door, the guy went over to one of the girls and chatted for a while. Then he went back to his wife.

"Was that girl you were talking to your

tilot?" she asked.

He nodded.

"Are all of these girls *tilots*?" she asked, looking around the club.

He nodded.

"You know what," she continued, "I like *ours* the best."

Probably bullshit.

Sam was so gorgeous that she attracted a lot of attention from the guys in the squadron. Instead of "Hey, Hamfist, if you get shot down, can I have your stereo gear?" it was, "Hey, Hamfist, if you get shot down, can I have your wife?"

When she was working at the Ubon JAG Office, Sam had heard my name mentioned. Apparently, I had gotten a reputation as "Mr. Suggestion".

It all started early in my tour, when we were

filling out some post-mission paperwork. One of the WSOs in our flight was pissed off.

“Look at this,” he said, holding up a Bomb Damage Assessment report form. “We have to fill out this fucking BDA form and put it in that in-basket over there, that uncontrolled basket, and it's there for anybody to see. Totally uncontrolled. BDA is classified. It's supposed to be controlled.”

“Well,” I countered, “why don't you fill out a Suggestion Program form and get the procedure changed?”

“I don't have time for that shit,” he responded. “Why don't you?”

So I did. I filled out a Suggestion Program form, with a recommendation that the BDA form be overprinted with “Classified When Filled Out”. The suggestion was accepted, the in-basket was changed to a locked box with a slot in the top for the forms. Intel had the key. And I received an award of $25. Easy money.

That started me on my way to completing over a dozen Suggestion Program forms, with awards ranging from souvenir coffee mugs to $100 checks.

The suggestion I was most proud of had its genesis when I'd heard Elm Three bail out, on my first Linebacker mission. He had gotten on his URC-64 survival radio while he was still in his chute, but we could hardly understand him because of the background noise from the wind. I wondered how we could arrange it so that we could attach our oxygen mask microphones to our URC-64s.

Our oxygen masks connected to the airplane oxygen system through the CRU-60/P connector on our parachute harness. On bailout, the aircraft oxygen hose would separate from the CRU-60/P connector, along with the oxygen mask microphone cord. The microphone cord would just be dangling from the CRU-60/P.

I figured there must be a way to connect that microphone cord to the URC-64 radio. The URC-64 did have a jack for an external microphone in its base, but that jack was a completely different size than the oxygen mask microphone connector.

I went to the radio shop and looked around at the different types of connectors they had. I found a U-41 male connector that fit the URC-64 radio, and a U-72 female connector that fit the oxygen mask microphone cord. I borrowed a soldering gun and hooked them together.

"It will never work, Captain," observed a Master Sergeant, "The impedance is all wrong. One is a dynamic mike, and the other is a carbon mike."

I knew something about impedance, since I had a degree in Electrical Engineering from the Academy. But I also knew not to let perfect be the enemy of good. I grabbed my contraption, the connector I had just built. I plugged one end into my URC-64, plugged the other end into my oxygen mask microphone, and headed to the screen room.

The screen room was a cage, built out of metal screening, that could be used to test radios without the signal being broadcast all over. The screen room was large enough to stand up in, and was used by radio technicians to test their equipment.

I tested my creation, and, to the amazement of the Sergeant, it worked! I knew that with mismatched impedance it would not be optimal, but I didn't need optimal. I just needed good enough.

“Sarge, what do I need to do to have your guys make one of these for every pilot in the wing?”

He shuffled around his desk for a minute and produced a work order request form.

“Fill this out, sir, and I'll take care of the rest.”

"Thank you, Sergeant."

I filled out a Suggestion Program form, and we had connectors attached to the URC-64 radios of every pilot in the wing within a week. And a few days later, one of our guys was shot down. He got on his URC-64 while he was still in the chute, and we could hear him perfectly, CAFB – Clear As A Fucking Bell. The satisfaction of that far surpassed the cash award I got for that suggestion.

It was great having Sam with me, for a lot of reasons. She was with me when I got up at 0130 to go back to the base for each Special. She saw the nervousness, the turmoil I went through before each mission. She met the guys in the squadron, my brothers. She went to squadron parties with me. And she grieved with me when we lost squadron-mates.

It was especially good for another reason. She had the war experience. She was mentally ready for whatever would happen to me. If I got shot down again, she wouldn't be caught off guard. The war became real to her. It made our relationship closer, much closer. We cherished every second we had together, and every moment of intimacy was more meaningful.

And then she had to leave. Her TDY was over, and she had to return to Yokota. I went with her to the Passenger Terminal and saw her off. This was a complete reversal of the roles we had previously served, where she watched me board flights.

As the plane taxied off, early in the morning, I was left with an empty feeling in the pit of my stomach, and I headed to work. I needed to be around people I knew.

When I arrived at the squadron, I saw Doc Myers talking to Lieutenant Colonel Smith. He was holding a magazine, and both of them were chuckling. As soon as he saw me, Lieutenant Colonel Smith called to me.

“Hey, Hamfist, get in here.”

"Good morning, sir, Doc. What's up?"

"You're famous," Doc Myers said, holding out a copy of *Aerospace Medicine Magazine*.

The lead article was about the 28-year-old pilot who had caught his testicles between his parachute harness and his body. As I read the article, I was shocked.

"Doc, you didn't tell me how close I was to requiring castration!"

"I didn't want to worry you, Hamfist. There was the real potential for necrosis with testicular torsion, but there was nothing you could do about it other than bed rest. That's why I insisted you stay off your feet. You looked fine during the follow-up, and I don't anticipate any reproductive problems in the future ."

"Thanks, Doc. Glad I could help you get published."

There was no Special this day. Instead, we had a squadron meeting at 0800, mandatory attendance.

Lieutenant Colonel Smith stood up in front of the squadron and made the announcement.

"Gentlemen, Operation Linebacker has ended."

Total silence. You could have heard a mouse fart. I had mixed emotions. I was really glad there would be no more Specials. I wouldn't have to look at the guys in the briefing room and wonder which of them – or me – wouldn't be returning. At the same time, I already had 69 missions over the North, and I really wanted to get that coveted 100 mission patch. And I wanted another chance at a MiG. Stupid, really.

Slowly, people started talking, softly. Then, someone in the back of the room started clapping, and then the whole room erupted in wild applause.

"We'll still be flying combat missions over Laos, Cambodia and South Vietnam, so don't go and get careless, but there will be no more bombing missions north of the twentieth parallel," he continued. "And, we've got a few good-deal missions scheduled. You'll see them on the scheduling board after 0900."

We all hung around the Scheduler's office like hawks, waiting for the day's schedule to be finalized. I lucked out. I would be taking an airplane to Clark Air Base, in the Philippines, for a much-needed IRAN – Inspect And Repair As Necessary. The Maintenance folks at Ubon didn't have the facilities to do IRAN, but the team at Clark did. IRAN would take about three days, so we would be totally off-duty, and collecting TDY pay, for three days. A paid vacation.

I was paired up with Deacon again. Deacon and I were scheduled to leave at 1500 for an easy 3-hour flight. The aircraft had a baggage pod loaded centerline, and we could easily get our B-4 bags into it, with plenty of room to bring back any souvenirs we may find at Clark.

It was dark when we arrived at Clark. This was the first mission I had flown in a long time with no munitions, and it was a funny feeling not needing to go to the de-arm area after landing. We turned our airplane over to Maintenance, and headed to Chambers Hall, the new Billeting Office.

Unlike all the other BOQs I had stayed at in the past, we were given individual rooms. And these were new rooms, not the old World War Two-era barracks I had seen during my previous trip to Clark, when I had attended Snake School. There was a color television in my room, and I even had a coffee maker. I told Deacon I'd meet him in the lobby in about a half-hour to go to the O'Club, and I flipped on the television.

There were only a few channels available, and they were all controlled by the Philippine government. President Marcos – no relation to Tom – had declared Martial Law about a month earlier, and the government controlled everything. Up until last month, pretty much every Filipino male had a knife or gun in his back pocket.

Now, guns were outlawed. Government soldiers were making house-to-house searches for guns, drugs and other contraband. Anyone caught with a gun would be immediately taken out and, in the words of the government spokesman, “executed by musketry”. As I was watching the local program that was on the television, the scene switched to a live camera shot.

“We interrupt this program,” the announcer said, “to show you the execution of Juan Verara. Mr. Verara was found to have a gun hidden in his house.”

Mr. Verara, an ordinary-looking Filipino about 25 years old, was brought outside and made to stand against a wall. His hands were tied behind his back. Then there was the sound of a bunch of rifle shots, and he fell down dead.

No “ready, aim, fire”. One minute he was alive, now he was dead.

The program went back to the soap opera, or whatever had been showing. Life in the Philippines went back to normal.

Except, of course, for the family of Mr. Verara.

62

October 26, 1972

Three days at Clark Air Base made for a nice break from Ubon. They had a great BX, and the O'Club was much nicer than the one we had at Ubon.

Deacon and I went out to some nice small restaurants in Angeles City, right outside the base. We discovered a great local dish, called *lumpia*. Basically, *lumpia* was an egg roll with jalapeno peppers inside. Certainly not bland, but not too spicy, especially when washed down with a cold San Miguel beer.

We were told to be ready to fly back to Ubon in the afternoon. I had breakfast in the O'Club, then returned to my room and turned on the television, just in time to see a news flash. Henry Kissinger appeared on the screen. He was in Paris at the Peace Talks with North Vietnam.

“Peace is at hand,” Kissinger intoned in his heavy accent.

This was fantastic news. The POWs would be coming home soon. Maybe we would find out what happened to Vince. I was ecstatic.

Fuck the hundred missions over the North. Fuck the MiG-kill. I wanted this fucking war to end.

63

December 18, 1972

The war, of course, wasn't over. Now it was a different war, with no missions north of the twentieth parallel. But we still had plenty of combat. And guys still got shot down.

One of the squadrons had been flying only missions over Pack Six, and they had a dry period for several weeks until they could get additional taskings for missions in Laos. In fact, some of their guys were losing their combat pay and their tax exemptions.

Since we were based in Thailand, we didn't get combat pay, a few hundred dollars a month extra, if we didn't fly combat. Just as important, we only received an exemption from paying income tax during any month we got combat pay. It all added up to a significant amount.

During this dry spell, there was still a way to

get combat pay, by flying in combat with one of the other squadrons. Some of their guys were temporarily assigned to our squadron for a mission or two, while some of them volunteered to fly on Specter AC-130 gunship missions.

The gunship missions were strictly boondoggles for the fighter guys, where the F-4 jocks rode along as observers, with no actual mission duties. But they were on the flight orders, they were in combat, and they got combat pay and tax exemption. After the first of November, when they still hadn't flown any combat missions, several of the F-4 guys volunteered for Specter missions. The Specters could only take one extra observer at a time, so as November wore on, there was a rush to get a Specter ride.

Then a Specter got shot down over the Plain des Jarres, in Laos. There was an F-4 jock on board. A Jolly Green was dispatched to the PDJ and made contact with some survivors. One of the AC-130 crewmembers verified that he had bailed out and had come down near the F-4 jock. The jock had landed in the trees, and then the branch holding his parachute had broken. The jock fell to the ground and then the branch – a really heavy branch – had fallen on him, crushing his chest. By the time the AC-130 crewmember got to him, he was dead.

This was a wake-up call for us for several reasons. We were all made acutely aware that combat pay was there because we were doing something dangerous. We were in combat. And in combat, people get killed.

Perhaps more significantly, we became aware that the AC-130 mission was actually pretty damned dangerous. Up until now, we F-4 jocks had kind of ignored the Specter crews, because we flew over Hanoi and they didn't. We flew supersonic jets, while they flew big, lumbering propeller-driven airplanes. We were, in a word, arrogant. Specter getting shot down opened our eyes to their mission and the fact that they had a mission that was as dangerous and, yes, as important, as ours.

I didn't need to decide if I wanted to fly with Specter. I flew 29 missions between October 26th and December 18th. Nineteen of them were over North Vietnam, the area around Bat Lake and Fingers Lake. They were sensor implant missions, not bombing missions. And they were in southern North Vietnam. No SAMs. No MiGs. Only triple-A. This war was getting kind of easy.

We had a squadron party this night. It was a going-away party for a couple of our guys, and it was sort of an early Christmas party. We started at about 1700, and we all took turns telling funny stories about the guys who were getting ready to DEROS. We had just started drinking, and everyone was in a great mood.

It was my turn to tell a story about one of our back-seaters, a guy we called Papa Foxtrot. Papa Foxtrot was the phonetic alphabet for the letters P and F. When we weren't in the public eye, we called the guy Pig Fucker, because he was always going out with ugly girls. With so many beautiful girls in Thailand, he only found the ugly ones.

"We're really going to miss Papa Foxtrot because now we won't have anyone..." I was interrupted by the Wing Commander, who had just walked into the Club.

"Gentlemen, the party is over."

Most of us smiled, waiting for the punch line. The Colonel wasn't smiling. There was no punch line.

"There will be a mission briefing at 0400 tomorrow morning. Everyone will attend," he continued. "As I said, the party is now over."

We were all in shock as we filed out of the Club and back to our rooms. I set my alarm for 0230. I eventually got to sleep, but not before doing a lot of thinking. Wondering.

Two months ago, Kissinger had said peace was at hand. It was now almost Christmas. What the fuck had happened?

64

December 19, 1972

When I got to Intel, the mood was totally different than before, during Linebacker. The shoot-down board was filled with the names of crewmembers who had been shot down during the night. There weren't enough lines on the board, and some of the lines contained two names. And three of the airplane losses were B-52s, six crewmembers each.

This was about as incomprehensible as it could get. You just didn't send a B-52 over an area protected by SA-2s. A B-52 couldn't dodge a SAM the way an F-4 could. A B-52 was big. It was lumbering. It was not maneuverable.

We all gathered in the mass briefing auditorium. There was a large curtain covering the projection screen. The Wing Commander walked up to the front, and a hush enveloped the room.

"Gentlemen, last night Operation Linebacker Two was launched. One hundred twenty-nine B-52s attacked Hanoi last night, and our own night squadron pilots flew essential support missions, including MiG Cap."

"Your targets," he continued, "are in the Hanoi area."

As he spoke, the curtain opened and a map of downtown Hanoi was projected on the screen, with red triangles denoting our targets.

"Due to the monsoon weather, you probably will not be able to see your targets, so you will make level deliveries using the LORAN bombing system. You will each carry twelve Mark-82 dumb bombs."

"Gentlemen, this is an all-out war effort, and there will be no SAR until the war is over. If you get shot down, you are on your own until the war ends. I will be leading the initial wave. Are there any questions?"

A senior Captain raised his hand.

"Colonel, when we jink from MiGs and SAMs, the LORAN will give us a settle light. We won't be able to complete our deliveries."

"Let me make this perfectly clear to all of you. You will not jink or maneuver your aircraft until your bombs are released. You will not do anything that will give you a settle light."

Well, that took care of that. Now I understood the railroad tie mission. It was preparation for today. We went to our individual mission briefings with a sense of resignation. When three B-52s, with six crewmembers in each, get shot down, an individual F-4 didn't seem so important any more. If I needed to fly wings level over Hanoi to get my bombs on target, so be it.

As I walked back to the squadron for the mission brief, I thought about the motivational movies they had shown us at the Academy, during the summer of my first year, doolie summer. Every morning after drill practice, we would assemble in the base theater and watch training films to learn about the proud heritage of the Air Force.

One of the movies I remembered the most vividly was the inflight footage of the B-24 bombing mission against the German refineries at Ploesti, Romania. Fifty-three aircraft, with six hundred sixty crewmembers, were lost on that mission. The Ploesti raid suffered the worst Army Air Force single-mission loss of the entire war. Out of 178 B-24s, not one aircraft turned back due to enemy fire.

"I want to remind you all," the Wing Commander told us during the briefing, "there's never been an Air Force aircraft that has aborted its mission due to enemy reaction."

I was scheduled to be the airborne spare, Walnut Five. I had the lineup information for all of the flights, and I took off after they had all launched, joining up with Elm Flight, the last flight to take off. I tagged along with Elm

Flight, and took on fuel with them on the tanker.

At tanker drop-off, when none of the strike aircraft had air aborted, I checked in with Hillsboro, the Direct Air Support Center, and they assigned me to work with a FAC in Laos. I had great bombs, with several secondaries, and then RTB'd to Ubon.

And I waited for the return of my comrades.

65

December 20, 1972

I was Number Four in Bronco flight. This was an unusual call sign, since most of our strike flights on the Specials were named after trees: Maple, Elm, Walnut, Beech. Our target was a radar and communications center, north of Hanoi.

More B-52s had been shot down during the night, and Guard frequency was cluttered with survivors calling for help and some replies by SAR aircraft. Apparently, there was still SAR activity, but only in Laos. None in North Vietnam.

As we got over Hanoi, I put the light on the star and ignored the sounds coming from my RHAW gear and the shadows that flitted in and out of my peripheral vision. I could discern a couple of airbursts, likely SAMs, that had missed us. A few hundred yards on the other side of Lead I saw an air-to-air missile go by in the opposite direction. But I didn't look around, like I usually did. I was capable of flying fingertip formation and still looking around, but I chose not to. I had briefed Deacon to not call out any MiGs or SAMs until after we delivered our bombs. If I couldn't maneuver to avoid a threat, I didn't even want to know about it.

As we ingressed the target area, I could see that it was completely undercast. The bomb deliveries really needed to be LORAN deliveries, or nothing at all.

Lead came over the radio.

"Bronco Flight, three, two, one, pickle, pickle, pickle."

As soon as he said "pickle" I pressed my pickle button, and my bombs fell in close formation with Lead's. Then we all immediately spread out to tactical formation, looking for threats. I was hoping we'd see a

MiG. We all had AIM-7 Sidewinder radar-guided missiles, and I think we all wanted a little mano-a-mano action.

No such luck.

66

December 23, 1972

I was fragged on a single-ship flight to implant sensors for the Igloo White program just north of the Demilitarized Zone. This was my ninety-first mission over the North. I was carrying Adsids and Accusids, seismic and acoustic sensors that looked like artificial Christmas trees. They were carried in a SUU-40 dispenser, and my run-in was going to be at tree-top level, with a pop-up to 1000 feet for the actual delivery. Although my target was north of the twentieth parallel, it was not a bombing mission, so it was permitted.

As I crossed the DMZ into North Vietnam and started my descent for the run-in, I saw a silver airplane maneuvering over Fingers Lake. I had been briefed that there were no friendly aircraft in the area, and this looked like it might be a MiG. I could feel my pulse pounding in my temples against my helmet padding as my excitement mounted.

I switched over to Hillsboro frequency.

"Hillsboro, this is Nile."

"Go ahead, Nile."

"Roger, I have a visual with a silver aircraft over Fingers Lake, just north of the DMZ. Are there any friendly aircraft in the area?"

"Negative, Nile. Go get 'em!"

"Roger. Wilco."

My fangs were really out now. I unloaded to about a half-G and lit minimum burner. I was closing fast and had a good aspect ratio on the target aircraft. I put my pipper on the target and hit the AUTO-ACQ button on the throttle quadrant, to get a good radar lock-on. I armed up my AIM-7 missiles and performed a low-speed yo-yo.

I was closing fast, and would be within firing range in another second. Two at the most. I had a good visual on the enemy, and got a good ID on him. It was a MiG, red star on the tail and all. I was going to fire both AIM-7s in rapid succession. Even if one didn't guide, the other one probably would. My finger tightened on the trigger.

Suddenly, the radar screen turned black, with a giant red "X" across its face.

"Don't fire! Don't fire!" My WSO was screaming on the intercom.

And then, a funny thing happened. I blinked, and the MiG, with the red star on the tail, instantly turned into a U.S. Navy A-7. Instantly.

I had wanted it to be a MiG so badly, it had become a MiG, reality be damned.

And, all of a sudden, I understood how, every year, hunters go out and shoot cows, horses, even cars, convinced they were firing at deer.

67

December 27, 1972

After almost shooting down the Navy plane, four days earlier, I almost "bought the farm" – a euphemism for getting killed – on that very mission. The Igloo White mission required the single-ship pilot to make his delivery from 1000 feet above the target, rock-steady for the full 30 seconds it took for the artificial trees to come out of the back of the SUU-40 dispenser.

Thirty seconds could seem like a lifetime. There would be plenty of time for the gomers to see you, acquire you as a target, and fire their triple-A or heat-seeking SA-7 missiles, the same missile that had shot me down three years earlier.

About the only way to protect yourself on the delivery was to make the ingress at treetop level and then pop up to 1000 feet at the last possible second. At least that way the gomers would have less reaction time. And then, right after the delivery, you had to either climb like a bat out of hell, or hit the deck one more time.

I had opted for the latter. As soon as the last sensor had left the airplane, I lit minimum burner, pushed over and headed for the treetops. My altimeter read “zero’, and my radar altimeter, when I looked at it, which wasn’t often, read 10 feet. I was flying strictly by outside references, headed to the coast to get feet wet as quickly as I could.

And then I felt the airplane start to pitch down, ever so slightly. I pulled back, gently, on the stick, and the airplane started pitching up. It went through several of these slow oscillations, and I gradually increased my altitude to about 50 feet. Suddenly, I saw a small black object flick past my aircraft so fast I almost didn’t see it. It had been a bird. If I had collided with it, my plane would have vaporized.

Finally we were feet wet, and I pointed the plane skyward and exited the threat envelope. For the life of me, I couldn't figure out what had caused the aircraft to porpoise when I was down low.

"Were you on the controls with me when we were down in the weeds?" I asked my WSO.

"No way, Hamfist. If we got in a fighting match on the controls at that altitude, it would have been all over."

Then it occurred to me what had happened. I remembered the aeronautics lesson at RTU where they had talked about Mach Tuck. I had been operating in the transonic region, and had been experiencing Mach Tuck, at 10 feet above the ground! As the airplane accelerated, we got Mach Tuck. The drag of the SUU-40 dispenser was so high, that we couldn't remain supersonic for very long, and the aircraft decelerated. That was what caused the pitch up.

Flying transonic at that altitude was a really stupid thing to do, for several reasons. First, obviously, was Mach Tuck. Just as important, the potential for bird strikes. And finally, I had been operating in excess of the speed limit of the SUU-40 dispenser. Real dumb on all three counts.

I had another opportunity to get a MiG, a real one this time. I was scheduled to be Card Three, the element lead for Card Flight. We were fragged as Quick Reaction Force.

The QRF crews would preflight their airplanes, then sit around the squadron until the klaxon went off. That's what we did. We had been briefed that we may be needed for a pop-up SAR if the opportunity presented itself. Even though the Wing Commander had said there would be no SARs in North Vietnam, there was the possibility it might occur, if conditions were just right. That's why we were on the QRF.

The klaxon went off, and we sprinted to our planes. Quick start, check-in, taxi and takeoff. Five, maybe six minutes had transpired between klaxon and gear up.

We were carrying CBU-24s and Mark-82s. Perfect munitions for a SAR. As we headed north, we refueled on Green anchor and switched over to strike frequency. Apparently, someone had heard a beeper in the Hanoi area, and we were being sent in to provide air cover if a SAR was launched. We set up a racetrack over Thud Ridge and waited.

After a while, we needed to refuel, and headed back to Green Anchor. We ended up doing this orbit-refuel-orbit dance several times. We didn't hear any beepers on Guard. Just silence.

But then, Disco, the Airborne Warning And Control System aircraft, came up on strike frequency. AWACS aircraft had sophisticated equipment, as well as linguists, on board. They knew whenever a MiG took off, and they frequently knew who was flying it. They would give enemy aircraft – bandit – locations relative to downtown Hanoi, called “bulls-eye”.

“Card flight, bandits, bull’s-eye 280 for 15, headed north.”

Our formation turned to face the bandits. I saw the missile one of the MiGs had fired before I saw the MiGs. It came toward us and harmlessly detonated well short of our position. But, fortunately, the missile smoke trail helped direct my eyes toward the MiGs.

The MiGs were now maneuvering, and Lead called for us to jettison our bombs and arm up our missiles. I reached over to the left sidewall Missile Status panel, turned the selector to Left Wing and pressed the PUSH TO JETTISON button, then turned it to the Right Wing position and pressed again. Now I had a clean wing. I reached down and moved my Master Arm switch to ARM.

We were in a hard turn, in spread formation, when Lead lost sight of the MiGs.

"Card Lead has lost sight of the target. Card Three, do you have the target in sight?"

"Affirmative," I answered.

"Roger, Card Three, you have the lead."

This was what I had fantasized about for years. I was finally leading a four-ship formation in a dogfight over North Vietnam. This time I was going to get my MiG. I performed a high-speed yo-yo, and closed near a firing position. No lock-on yet, but any second.

And then, the MiGs disappeared into the sun.

It was the oldest trick in the book, used ever since World War One. I had lost the MiGs in the sun.

There is an old expression fighter pilots learn.

“If you lose sight of your enemy, don't worry. Just wait a few seconds and look at your six o'clock.”

If I had been single-ship, I might have stayed in the fight. Fuck it, better a MiG at six o'clock than no MiG at all. But not when I have three wingmen depending on me to make the right decision. I did a quarter-roll and disengaged.

“Card Three has lost the target. Card One, you have the lead.”

We headed for home base. We had jettisoned our bombs, and couldn't do anyone any good now. We had flown for almost six hours, and hadn't accomplished a fucking thing. We sure hadn't helped anyone on a SAR.

And, once again, I had blown my chance to get a MiG.

68

December 30, 1972

There was no Special this day. We were launched on a dumb bomb mission over South Vietnam, near the DMZ.

Guard frequency was constantly cluttered with calls from survivors who had been shot down during the previous several days, and I turned off the Guard receiver just to be able to communicate on strike frequency. The other aircraft in our formation, Redtop Flight, did the same thing. I found out shortly that turning off Guard hadn't been a very good idea.

As a nice change, I was Number Two. We were working with an OV-10 FAC, and had set up a left wheel over the target. Unlike a typical airstrike with a FAC, where the target is somewhat concealed, our target today was sticking out like a sore thumb. It was a massive POL storage area north of Quang Tri that had belonged to the friendlies. POL was the acronym for Petroleum, Oil, Lubricant. In other words, it was fuel storage.

The ARVN, the South Vietnamese Army, was in the process of a frantic retreat from the advancing NVA, the North Vietnamese Army. Sorry, my mistake. Not a retreat, a retrograde advance. Our job was to bomb the POL to prevent it from falling into enemy hands.

The FAC didn't even need to mark the target. He simply described it, and we started our attack. Lead had just pulled off target, and I was rolling in for my delivery. Suddenly, the ground beneath my aircraft erupted in a series of massive explosions, spread over a huge area that encompassed much more than just our target. And I saw bombs, a lot of bombs, falling past my aircraft.

I rolled wings level and looked overhead. There, well above me, was a line of B-52s in trail formation, about a mile apart. And I could see bombs falling down toward my aircraft. Small bombs that got larger and appeared to move further apart as they descended above me. It was reminiscent of looking up during a light drizzle, when you can see the individual raindrops, slowly appearing to spread further apart.

There was no way to jink to avoid the bombs. I could just as easily have jinked into a bomb as away from it. I immediately thought of another of the motivational movies I had seen at the Academy, the movie that contained inflight footage of a high-altitude bomb run where one of the B-24s had gotten out of position. A bomb from an airplane above him had gone right through his wing, knocking him out of the sky. Then I thought about what Boss Boston had told me when I was an FNG at DaNang – it's a big sky – and hoped it was still true. It would be bad enough to be shot down by the gomers. It would really be a bitch to be knocked down by a B-52.

Redtop Lead was screaming on the radio.

“Redtop Flight, exit the target area to the west. We'll rejoin at angels 15. Head west immediately!”

We all got the hell out of Dodge as fast as we could. We rejoined well west of the target area. All of us except Lead were unexpended, and we switched over to Hillsboro frequency and got a target and FAC in Laos to work with. None of us had very good bombs. I think we were all pretty shook up.

In retrospect, turning off our Guard receivers had been a really bad idea. Before every Arc Light B-52 strike, there was a warning on Guard five minutes before the strike, giving the target location and TOT. It was the FAC's responsibility to know about any nearby airstrikes, but he probably had Guard punched off also.

We all learned a lot on that mission.

69

January 2, 1973

This mission, Confine Flight, was another dumb bomb mission, this time to a target in Laos. I was Number Two in the flight, and we were working with a Covey FAC, Covey 114.

As soon as we made our rendezvous, I knew where we were. Precisely. I instantly recognized the white cliffs of Delta 43, the target area where I had gotten shot down the first time during my FAC tour out of DaNang. The target area where I had gotten in a life-or-death duel with a 9-level gunner and won.

I was ecstatic! I wanted to get on the radio and say, "Hey, Covey, I was a Covey here three years ago. I killed a 9-level gun here!"

But I didn't. Flight discipline required that I keep my mouth shut unless there was an operational requirement to transmit. Maybe someday, at some sort of FAC reunion, I would swap war stories. But today, I only said, “Two's in from the east.”

Our target was two tanks, completely out in the open. We had 12 Mk-82s on each airplane, and lead killed the east-most tank. I rolled in and pickled off four bombs. Correction, I selected four bombs for release.

After my delivery, I rolled into a sharp right bank to see my bombs hit. My first bomb hit about twenty meters short of the target, directly on the run-in line. The second bomb hit ten meters short. Then there was a pause, and my last bomb hit ten meters long. I had a hung bomb, and the bomb that had hung was the one that would have been a perfect hit. Boy, was I pissed!

I re-homed my MER and came around for another run to see if the hung bomb would release. It did, and it landed directly on the tank.

The tanks were all killed, and we put the

remainder of our bombs on some storage areas, and got a few good secondaries.

It was another really great mission.

70

January 9, 1973

I was launched as Wolf 32, teamed up with Fast FAC Wolf 31. The recent spate of Fast FACs being shot down had required a change of plans. Now, every Fast FAC would have a FAC escort. My job, basically, was to stay out of the way while Wolf 31 conducted airstrikes, and I would serve as the on-scene commander if and when Wolf 31 got shot down.

If Wolf 31 found a lucrative target and could not get any other air support, he was permitted to use my ordnance. The risk, though, was that he might employ all of my munitions and then get shot down, and I wouldn't have any ordnance to support his SAR.

On this mission, Wolf 31 found a lot of targets, and put in several sets of fighters. I orbited high and stayed out of everyone's way, and when Wolf 31 went to the tanker to refuel,

I went with him and topped off also.

When we went back to the area around Bat Lake, Wolf 31 found a truck speeding down a route segment. It wasn't worth calling for an entire four-ship of F-4s for a solitary truck, so he decided to put me in on the truck.

“Wolf 32, do you have that truck, or do I need to mark it?”

“I have the truck in sight,” I answered. I wasn't blind!

“Okay, 32, I want you to run in from north to south with one CBU-24. I'll be holding off to the east. You're cleared in hot.”

I armed up to drop just one CBU-24 and rolled in. I was a bit steep, and I released a little below the planned release point.

Okay, I released a *lot* below the planned release altitude. As I pulled off target, I rolled up and looked for the tell-tale flash indicating that the radar fuse in the CBU had opened the clam-shell case. No flash. Shit! I had released too low. The radar fuse on the CBU needed to see 4500 feet above ground to open the clam-shell. Now the CBU would hit unopened.

The ballistics for an unopened CBU clam-shell were totally different than the ballistics for a properly delivered CBU. The mills setting I had used for my bomb sight wouldn't even be close to correct. A totally wasted CBU.

Then an amazing thing happened. The unopened CBU scored a direct hit on the truck. Landed *directly* in the truck bed, and exploded like a 750-pound bomb. There were huge secondaries. Wolf 31 was ecstatic.

“Shit hot, Wolf 32! I told you to drop a CBU, but your Mark-82 was perfect. Absolutely perfect!”

I wasn't about to tell him that he had just witnessed the most incredible series of compensating errors of the entire war. I just let him think I drop *really great* bombs! I'd rather be lucky than good any day.

Right after the truck attack, two 37 mike mike guns opened up on us. Wolf 31 put me in on them with my CBUs and what he thought was the remainder of my Mark-82s. We killed both guns, and got seven secondary fires.

We hit the tanker one last time, and then RTB'd to Ubon.

I didn't correct Wolf 31 when he told all of the guys what great bombs I had.

71

January 13, 1973

This was a big day for me. I was Number Two in Godson Flight. Lead had a Pave Way Zot Box, and would illuminate our target, a pontoon bridge. I was carrying 2 Mk-84Ls. A pontoon bridge is as nitnoy as you can get. That's not the reason it was a big day.

This was my 100th mission over North Vietnam.

I had great bombs, we had no enemy reaction to speak of, and the war over the north was officially scheduled to end in two days. When I landed, I felt like a big weight had been lifted from my shoulders, kind of like the feeling I'd get every time I removed my heavy survival vest at the end of each mission. I had achieved one of my goals.

I think – but I can't prove – I was the last Air Force pilot to get 100 missions over the north. All flying north of the 20th parallel ended on January 15, 1973.

I had been lucky, really lucky.

72

January 17, 1973

There were a couple of interesting, unrelated events that occurred shortly after the war over the north ended. One happened the night after the bombing halt.

One of the F-4s from the night squadron had been launched to rendezvous with a Spector C-130 gunship over the Plain des Jarres, in Laos, to serve as an escort. The Specs often drew ground fire, and it helped to have a fighter overhead with some heavy ordnance if it was needed. Typically, the escort would orbit high above the gunship, and if anything opened up on the Spector, the fighter would roll in on them.

Hooking up with the Spector consisted of getting refueled on Green anchor while heading north, then doing a 45-degree left heading change at tanker drop-off, which would aim the aircraft directly at the PDJ. Then, at the appropriate time, after comparing radial and DME from a known TACAN station, the F-4 would find the Spector.

On this particular night, the F-4 pilot was probably pretty tired, and he made a mistake. Given the right, actually, wrong, circumstances, I suppose I could have done it myself.

Instead of turning 45 degrees *left*, the pilot turned 45 degrees *right*. That took him directly over Hanoi. Not a shot was fired. The gomers were probably wondering *what the fuck is this guy doing?* The WSO apparently didn't pick up the error either. Not until the pilot spoke.

“The moon sure is pretty reflecting off the water.”

“WHAT WATER?! THERE'S NO FUCKING WATER IN THE PLAIN DES JARRES!”

That's when the crew realized where they were. By this time, the gomers probably figured that this crew would be in deeper shit when they landed than anything they could possibly do to them.

So, no shots were fired, the crew turned around and RTBd, and, other than bruised egos, no harm done.

The second event involved our squadron scheduler, Cobra Corbin. Cobra was a really sharp Captain. He had completed all of his Professional Military Education, his PME. A lot of us considered PME just so much busy-work, but Cobra was really into it. He had completed Squadron Officer School and Air Command and Staff School by correspondence while he was at Ubon. He had great Officer Effectiveness Reports. He was a great pilot. He had great military bearing. He was so sharp that he had just been selected as Junior Officer of the Year. Truly a real honor. Hell, he even beat me for the Junior Officer of the Year Award!

Well, on this daytime flight, Cobra was flying as a fast FAC, Wolf 51, on a mission over Laos.

His escort was Wolf 52. It was a slow day, and he hadn't found any targets. Hillsboro called him and advised him that there was a report of a beeper in the Hanoi area. They wanted him to fly over Hanoi and see if he could raise any survivors on the radio.

Although there was a bombing halt over North Vietnam, aircraft could still fly there if directed, as was this case. Cobra and his wingman headed north.

When they got over Hanoi, there was no enemy reaction, and the entire area was undercast. Cobra lit his burner a few times, to try to attract the attention of any survivor who might be on the ground. Nobody came up on the radio. Then Cobra got a bright idea.

"Wolf, 52, I want you to drop one Mk-82. That will make enough noise to let any survivor know we're here."

Wolf 52 dutifully dropped one 500-pound bomb, in level flight, through the undercast.

Still, no one came up on the radio. After about a half-hour, Wolf Flight RTBd to Ubon.

That one bomb had just put the Paris Peace Talks in peril. The negotiators had heard about it within minutes. Kissinger had phoned Nixon to tell him about it. Nixon, Nixon himself, had phoned the new Wing Commander, to chew his ass out personally. The new Wing Commander, Colonel Nelson, was waiting for Wolf 51 Flight when they returned. He was waiting for Cobra.

"Captain Corbin," Colonel Nelson said, "I noticed your wingman is missing one Mark 82. What happened to it?"

"We dropped it on a target of opportunity in Laos, sir. Why do you ask?"

With that, Colonel Nelson exploded. His face turned red. The veins in his neck popped out. His eyes had become slits.

"You son of a bitch! You single-handedly ruined the fucking Paris Peace Talks! I'm going to have you court-martialed! I'm going to take your wings and shove them up your ass! I'm going to rip your fucking head off and shit down your neck!"

Cobra stood at attention and took it like a man. Then he responded in a way that made him a legend in his own time.

"Sir," he asked, "does this mean I'm no longer Junior Officer of the Year?"

73

February 12, 1973

This was the best day of the war.

The POWs were heading for home.

Operation Homecoming consisted of three C-141s that flew to Hanoi to pick up the first group of the 591 POWs that would be released. The *Stars & Stripes* published all of their names, and everybody in the squadron carefully scanned the list to see if there were any names we recognized. And pretty much all of us saw it at the same time: Vince and Sambo were both listed as returning POWs!

And then I saw the most remarkable, moving scene of my entire career. For all of our swagger and braggadocio, we fighter jocks were just a bunch of pussies. We were all crying, and all trying to hide it from each other. There wasn't a dry eye in the squadron.

Flying was cancelled for the day, and we headed to the bar. We all walked in wearing our hats, and we offered up a solemn toast to our 1350 comrades who were still missing.

74

March 15, 1973

The war, of course, continued on. We had missions over South Vietnam, Laos and Cambodia. I flew 23 additional missions after completing my 100 over the north.

This was my champagne flight, carrying 6 Mk-82s for a target in Cambodia. I was Number Two in Hoofer Flight of two aircraft. The plan was to deliver our ordnance, then we would RTB to base and split up. In the tradition of champagne flights, I would make a high-speed pass down the runway, then pull up into a closed pattern, land and taxi up to the Wing Headquarters building to get hosed down and presented with a bottle of champagne.

That was the plan. The reality was, just as we entered the target area my left engine rolled back to Idle power. I couldn't perform a weapons delivery, and held high while Lead dropped his bombs. I had to RTB without dropping any bombs, and the unexpended ordnance, plus the single-engine approach, required me to make a straight-in approach and landing, and an Approach End Barrier Engagement. No high-speed pass.

In a way, it was a good thing. I had never made an AEBE before, and it's something every fighter jock should experience at least once. The Navy jocks do it for a living. It turned out to be a non-event.

I de-armed and taxied to Wing Headquarters. Someone had gotten my mission statistics from Scheduling and written them on a large cardboard sign: 190 missions total, 100 over North Vietnam.

We had the obligatory picture-taking, the hose-down, the champagne.

It was really good to be done, and I couldn't wait to get home to Sam.

75

March 17, 1973

My follow-on assignment was to an F-4C squadron at Kadena Air Base, in Okinawa. The “poor man’s Hawaii”. Sam had a joint spouse assignment to Kadena also. I had requested, and received, two weeks of leave before traveling to Kadena.

Sam was waiting for me at the Yokota Passenger Terminal. When I walked through the Terminal door, Sam ran up to me, wrapped her arms around me and gave me a passionate kiss. God, I loved the way she always welcomed me home!

During the latter part of my tour at Ubon, I had stopped writing about operational issues, mostly because I didn't want Sam to worry. Now I couldn't wait to tell her that Vince had been released, that I had come close to getting a MiG, that I had reached the magic hundred missions.

“I have a lot to tell you, honey.”

“I have something to tell you also,” she responded.

“Okay,” I replied, “you go first.”

Sam grabbed both of my hands and looked into my eyes. “Ham, you're about to become a father. I'm pregnant.”

The adventure continues . . .

Follow the adventures of Hamfist Hancock here at:

www.GENolly.com

www.HamfistAdventures.com

Stay in touch with the author via:

Twitter: http://twitter.com/gnolly

If you liked *Hamfist Over Hanoi*, please post a review on Amazon.

Other books by G.E.Nolly:

Hamfist Over The Trail

Hamfist Down!

Happy Hancock

This Is Your Captain Speaking: Insider Air Travel Secrets

This Is Your Captain Speaking: Layover Security For Road Warriors

ABOUT THE AUTHOR

George Nolly served as a pilot in the United States Air Force, flying 315 combat missions on two successive tours of duty in Vietnam, flying O-2A and F-4 aircraft. In 1983, George received the Tactical Air Command Instructor of the Year Award for his service as an instructor in the Air Force Forward Air Controller Course. Following his Air Force duty, he hired on with United Airlines and rose to the position of B-777 Check Captain. He also served as a Federal Flight Deck Officer. Following his retirement from United, George accepted a position as a B-777 Captain with Jet airways, operating throughout Europe, Asia and the Middle East. In 2000, George was selected as a Champion in the Body-for-LIFE Transformation Challenge, and is a Certified Fitness Trainer and self-defense expert with more than 30 years' experience in combative arts. George received a Bachelor of Science Degree from the United States Air Force Academy and received a

Master of Science Degree, in Systems Management, from the University of Southern California. He completed all of the required studies for a second Master of Science Degree, in Education, at the University of Southern California, and received his Doctor of Business Administration Degree, specializing in Homeland Security, from Northcentral University. He now flight instructs in the B777 and B787.

Made in the USA
San Bernardino, CA
27 June 2013